D0175332

The Christmas Cat

Other Books by Melody Carlson

Christmas at Harrington's

The Christmas Bus

The Christmas Shoppe

The Joy of Christmas

The Treasure of Christmas

The Christmas Pony

A Simple Christmas Wish

The Christmas Cat

MELODY CARLSON

Revell
a division of Baker Publishing Group
Grand Rapids, Michigan

Published by Revell
a division of Baker Publishing Group
P.O. Box 6287, Grand Rapids, MI 49516-6287
www.revellbooks.com

Printed in the United States of America

Library of Congress Cataloging-in-Publication Data is on file at the Library of Congress, Washington, DC.

ISBN 978-0-8007-1966-1

14 15 16 17 18 19 20 7 6 5 4 3 2 1

Dedicated to Harry,
a very fine Maine Coon cat
who found us in the middle of a snowy winter
and won a place in all our hearts

1

Garrison Brown had been known to cross the street in order to avoid contact with a common house cat. As he hurried through the chilly Seattle air, he grimaced to see a black cat cut in front of him. With head down, the scrawny creature ducked into the alley behind a popular restaurant and disappeared into the mist. Garrison hated cats. Okay, *hate* was too strong a word. He simply wanted nothing to do with the furry little beasts.

During his missionary stint in Africa, his grandmother had lovingly teased him via email. "*Did you travel halfway across the globe just to escape my furry felines?*" For sure, domesticated cats were rare in Uganda, but it was not his cat allergies that had compelled him to leave the country—and Gram knew it.

As he went inside the apartment building where he'd secured temporary lodging with an old friend, Garrison reminded himself that cats could actually be rather amusing—from a safe distance anyway. He'd even enjoyed some of the hilarious YouTube videos that Gram had forwarded him over recent years. The one with the cat dressed as a shark riding a robot vacuum cleaner and pursuing a bird stood out in his mind.

It was impressive that his elderly grandmother had gotten so handy at technology, he thought as he scaled the first flight of creaky stairs. Equally amazing that the old girl had managed to accumulate so many cats during his nine years in Uganda. For some reason Gram had turned into a magnet for abandoned and abused cats. She called it her "St. Francis ministry," but he cringed to think of all those furry critters crawling about her home.

Garrison was well aware that Gram wasn't the only cat-loving person in this country. Unless it was his imagination, the country's cat population had hugely multiplied during his absence. He had no logical explanation for this phenomenon, but it seemed that everywhere he turned, including the ads on TV, there were cats, cats, cats. And he didn't mean the ones of the Broadway musical variety either!

He paused in the stairwell to dig his jangling phone from the depths of his coat pocket. Hoping it might be the director from the nonprofit agency he'd just interviewed with, he eagerly answered, "Hey, this is Garrison," with cheerful enthusiasm. His roommate had been encouraging him to sound younger and hipper—although Garrison was only thirty-four and not really ready to be put out to pasture. But according to Randall, Seattle was a youth-oriented town, and it seemed Garrison had some catching up to do—that is, if he wanted to fit in.

"Garrison Brown?" a deep voice asked.

"Yes, this is Garrison."

"I'm glad I could reach you, Garrison. Although I'm afraid I have some bad news."

Garrison's heart sank. The director had probably decided, like so many other personnel people, to politely decline him a job. Why was he even surprised? They didn't usually call back like this though.

"I'm Edward Miller," the man said. "I'm Lillian Brown's attorney and—"

"My *grandmother's* attorney?" Garrison interrupted. "Is something wrong?"

"Yes. I'm sorry to inform you that Mrs. Brown has passed away."

"Oh . . ." Garrison stopped climbing the stairs as a hard lump filled his throat. "Gram is dead?"

"Yes. She passed away this morning or maybe last night. A neighbor discovered her a few hours ago. I'm very sorry for your loss."

A heavy load of guilt pressed onto him. Garrison had truly meant to spend more time with his grandmother after returning from Uganda. He had *wanted* to. But with medical appointments to remedy his malaria . . . followed by job interviews to remedy his bank account . . . several months had passed and he'd only managed one visit down there so far and that was just one quick stop on a day trip with his roommate. He had planned to surprise her on Thanksgiving and spend the whole week with her. But now it was too late.

"What happened?" he asked weakly. "I mean, I realize she was in her late eighties, but she seemed in good health. I just talked with her a few days ago."

"I suspect it was her heart. Were you aware that she'd had some cardio problems?"

"No. She never mentioned it." He continued trudging up the last flight of stairs.

"Yes, well, she mentioned it to me late last summer. That's when she came in to make some changes regarding her estate. I suspect she knew that she wasn't long for this world."

"I had no idea. She always seemed so cheerful and energetic." Garrison felt tears filling his eyes as he pictured the old woman working in her garden . . . surrounded by her motley crew of castoff cats. He punched his fist against the door. Malaria or no malaria, why hadn't he spent more time with her right after he'd gotten home from Uganda?

"I'm sorry for your loss, Garrison. As I'm sure you must know, Mrs. Brown has designated you as her only heir."

Garrison sighed at the word *heir*. Poor Gram, like him, pretty much had nothing . . . besides her cats, that is. "Yes, well, Gram and I don't have many other relatives."

"So I'm hoping that you can come to Vancouver and help sort things—"

"Of course," Garrison agreed as he slid his key into the deadbolt of Randall's door. "I'll get down there as soon as possible. Maybe by tonight, if I can catch a bus in time."

"Tomorrow is soon enough." Mr. Miller gave some details regarding Gram's wishes for her funeral and interment. "I've already contacted her pastor. The service can be held next Monday at eleven, if you agree. But I'm sure there are some other details you'll want to attend to."

"Right." Garrison stepped into his friend's apartment, pausing to jot down some notes along with some phone numbers. "I'll call you when I get into town—probably tomorrow," he told the lawyer. They wrapped up the dismal conversation, then Garrison closed his phone and slumped into the well-worn leather recliner. Leaning forward with head in hands, he allowed his tears to flow. An old part of him felt ashamed—crying like this seemed unmanly. But then he remembered something a Ugandan friend once told him. "A real man is not afraid to shed tears." Besides, he reminded himself as he loudly blew his nose, this was Gram he was grieving.

Gram had been his rock after his parents were killed in a car wreck twenty-two years ago. She'd been recently widowed, but the older woman had shown real backbone by insisting on taking her bitter adolescent grandson into her home. She'd barely known Garrison at the time, and yet she had persistently loved him—through thick and thin. And there had been a lot of thin. But despite his deep-rooted rebelliousness and sassy back-talking habits, she refused to give up on him. She even forgave him when he nearly torched the nearby grade school. Her grace and diligence had eventually won him over—both to her and her faith. Without Gram he knew he would've gone down, or up, in flames.

And now she was gone and he couldn't even say goodbye.

"Hey, man." Garrison's roommate called out a greeting as he came into the apartment with a pair of grocery bags in his arms. "How'd the interview—" Randall's brow creased as he set a bag on the counter. "What's wrong?"

"My grandmother." Garrison sniffed and stood, squaring his shoulders, trying to act strong—manly. "Her lawyer just called. Gram passed away this morning."

"Oh, man, I'm so sorry." Randall sadly shook his head as he set down the other bag. "Your grandmother was one of the greats, you know. I've always had nothing but respect for that sweet woman. Too bad. But she had a good life. You know that, right?"

"Right." Garrison filled a glass with water, taking a big drink. "Gram was a real lady. I'm gonna miss her . . . a lot." He explained his plans to get a bus to Vancouver tomorrow morning.

"Or borrow my car," Randall said as he began unloading produce.

"Thanks. But I don't know how long I'll be down there. As far as I know, Gram never got rid of her old Pontiac. I'll just use that while I'm there."

"You're kidding. That car must be ancient by now."

"Yeah," Garrison agreed. "It was more than fifteen years old when the missions committee gave it to her after she came home from Kenya."

"Even so, it could really go. That was one big honking engine. Remember driving that car around when we were in high school?"

"Don't remind me." Garrison tried not to recall the times he'd driven too fast. "Anyway I'll just use it while I'm there—figuring stuff out." Garrison nodded to the array of foods that Randall was lining up along the counter. "What's up with all that?"

"I promised Rebecca I'd fix dinner tonight," Randall explained.

"Special occasion?"

Randall shrugged. "Nah. I just lost a bet."

"Well, I can make myself scarce if you two need to—"

"No way. You better stick around." His eyes lit up. "Besides, I'm making pad Thai. I know how much you like it."

Despite his gloom, Garrison's stomach rumbled. He

hadn't eaten since early this morning, and he remembered how Randall had worked his way through college cooking at a Vietnamese restaurant. His pad Thai was killer. "Need some help?" he offered.

"Sure." Randall handed him a bunch of green onions.

As they worked together, peeling and chopping, Garrison reminisced about Gram. "I remember when she took me in," he said. "She tried to hide it, but I could see that she was still grieving for my grandpa. He'd died just a few months earlier. That was a lot of sadness—losing her husband and her only son so close together like that. But she always seemed so strong. So faithful and optimistic."

"And hadn't she just come home from the mission field herself? My parents were on our church's mission committee at the time. I still remember them talking about this missionary widow and how everyone needed to help her feel at home in Vancouver."

"Yeah, she'd barely been moved back to the States. She'd wanted to stay in Kenya, to continue the work, but the mission board wouldn't allow it. Fortunately, for her and me too, my grandpa's parents had left that house to her."

"That was a good thing—for you and me both." Randall grinned as he poured some fish sauce into a measuring cup. "I remember when you guys moved into the neighborhood. I knew right away we were going to be best friends."

"Yeah. That was pretty cool." Garrison nodded as he scraped the chopped green onions into a metal bowl, then he sighed. "I still can't believe she's gone."

"At least you know she's in a better place."

Garrison sighed. "Yeah . . . but I wish I'd gone down to see her . . . I mean, before it was too late."

"Well, if anyone would understand, it would be your grandma. You gotta know she was really proud of you, man. Working in Uganda like you did. Helping to put all those wells into those villages." He grinned as he opened a jar of pepper paste. "She's probably up there in heaven, bragging on you right now."

Garrison made a weak half-smile as the doorbell rang and Randall hurried to answer it. Rebecca burst into the apartment, greeting Randall with her usual boisterous energy, exclaiming over the storm system that was pressing into the Sound. "Can you believe it was sixty degrees yesterday, but I heard a weather report saying we might have snow by Thanksgiving?" She waved at Garrison as she peeled off her parka.

Garrison had known Rebecca for nearly as long as he'd known Randall. They'd all gone to school together in Vancouver. But it was only recently that Randall and Rebecca had reconnected via social networking. They'd been dating steadily for nearly a month now. As a result, Garrison had begun to feel a bit like a third wheel around this place. Randall tried to play down the relationship, but Garrison felt certain that Rebecca was hearing wedding bells in her head. And seeing Randall greeting her with a kiss and whispering into her ear . . . Garrison knew it wasn't just Rebecca. Consequently, Garrison had been very focused on finding a job of late. He knew he needed to get out of here and onto his own two feet. The sooner the better for everyone. The problem was that the kind of jobs he was looking for were few and the applicants were many.

He dropped the last peeled carrot into the colander in the sink as he gave Rebecca an apologetic smile. "I didn't mean to crash your dinner party to—"

"You're *not* crashing," she declared as she came into the kitchen with sympathetic eyes. "Randall just told me about your grandmother." She gave him a warm hug. "I'm sorry, Garrison."

He just nodded. "Yeah. I know she was old and it sounds like she had some health problems, but I still can't believe she's gone."

"What will happen to all her cats?" Rebecca reached for a carrot, breaking it in half and taking a loud bite. "My aunt lives down the street from her house. Some of the neighbors—you know, the ones who don't know your grandma very well—they started calling her the Cat Lady. Rumor has it that she has like twenty cats now."

Garrison frowned. "Well, as far as I know, it was only seven at last count. No, make that six. Her oldest cat, Genevieve—that's the one she adopted right after I went to college—she died a couple months ago. I even sent Gram flowers. Genevieve was twenty-three years old."

"Seriously?" Randall took his place at the stove. "Cats really live that long?"

"I guess some do."

"They might call Gram the Cat Lady, but she definitely does not have twenty cats," Garrison clarified. "Well, unless she took in some other cats that I haven't heard about. Although we talked weekly. She never mentioned it."

"Well, six cats isn't so bad." Rebecca took another bite of carrot. "I saw this old woman on TV. She lived in Florida and had more than a hundred cats. All in one little house. Thankfully no one has invented smell-o-vision or I would've changed the channel. Seriously, it was disgusting."

Garrison shuddered. "Sounds nasty."

Rebecca laughed. "Yeah, especially for a cat-hater like you."

"Garrison doesn't *hate* cats," Randall said defensively. "It's just his allergies. I've seen him. A cat comes within ten feet of him and the poor guy starts sneezing and wheezing."

"I know, I know." Rebecca gave Garrison a contrite smile. "I just like to tease you."

The three of them chatted congenially as they worked together. Then they all sat down around a big bowl of pad Thai. After helping them clean up, Garrison excused himself to his room to make travel arrangements and pack some things. More than that, he wanted to be alone. And he was certain the couple wanted to be alone too. It seemed obvious that he didn't fit in here anymore. Sometimes he wondered if he fit in anywhere anymore. It was probably just a matter of time before those two decided to tie the knot. He really was happy for Randall. And Rebecca too. But he also felt like the odd man out. In so many ways.

Garrison wasn't really jealous. In fact, he was glad that Randall and Rebecca had found each other after all these years. They were all in their midthirties now. High time to settle down. If things had gone differently in Uganda, Garrison might've been married by this time too. But Leah had taken a different path—married someone else. And really, Garrison was over it. As Gram used to say, that was water under the bridge. He zipped up his packed duffle bag. No looking back.

Thinking of Gram again just brought all the sadness back. Why hadn't he gone home sooner? Were his excuses of job hunting and doctor visits really legitimate? Or had he secretly allowed a few old cats to keep him away? *Stupid cats!*

2

Rebecca had been right about the weather system pressing into the Seattle area. Ice-cold rain whipped against him as Garrison hurried to the bus station. It wasn't so much that he was unaccustomed to Washington's climate. But after the years in Uganda—and after suffering from malaria—he was having difficulty acclimating to the chilly, damp environment in the Northwest. Fortunately he'd had the forethought to layer on lots of clothes this morning. He probably looked like a refugee in his strange-looking ensemble. Not that he cared about fashion. Besides, for all practical purposes, he was homeless. Homeless, jobless, and alone.

He tried not to feel sorry for himself as the bus rumbled down I-5 toward Vancouver, Washington. Instead, he focused his thoughts on the sweet old house that he'd lived in from age twelve to graduation. It had been nothing like his parents' new home in a brand-new subdivision high on a hill. Gram's neighborhood, with old homes and tree-lined streets, had real personality. Sure the neighborhood had been a little run-down, but the people had been friendly. Of course, that could've changed by now. After all, he hadn't really spent time in that area during the past nine years. And his last visit, due to the cats, had been very brief. The truth was that Garrison hadn't really spent much time there since graduating from high school. That was more than sixteen years ago, and about the same time Gram had started taking in cats.

Garrison had understood when Gram had taken in her first cat. The big orange tabby she named Genevieve had seemed like good company for her. And Garrison knew that Gram had loved having cats as a child. He also knew that she grew very lonely when he left for college on the East Coast. He had actually been comforted to know she had Genevieve's companionship, and he'd told himself that he could simply take his allergy medicine whenever he came home. But over time his visits home grew rare. He claimed it was because of the cost of travel, but he knew it was also because of the cat. He learned quickly that visiting Gram for more than just a couple of hours put his health at risk. For her sake, though, he had tried to play it down. He never revealed to Gram that sometimes it felt as if she'd chosen the cat over him. He knew that would be selfish.

As Garrison walked from the downtown bus stop toward the old neighborhood, he noticed that some people were giving him curious glances. With his longish dark hair and layered clothes, beat-up duffle bag and backpack, he probably looked suspicious. The fact that he hadn't shaved probably didn't help much either. His plan was to drop off his bag, peel off some clothes, drive Gram's old Pontiac back to town for a quick bite, and then meet with the lawyer at two.

The neighborhood looked even more run-down than he remembered. Not only that, some of the trees had been cut down, giving it a stark and somewhat desolate appearance. And due to the chilly weather, no one was out and about. As he turned onto Gram's street, he wondered if she still kept a house key under the same flowerpot on the back porch. But if it wasn't there, he could always call on Ruby next door. Mr. Miller had mentioned she was seeing to Gram's cats, so Garrison knew she would have a key.

Gram's two-story white house still had the same sweet welcoming look at first glance, but as he got closer he could see that the paint was peeling and some of the shutters were sagging. He must've missed that when he'd dropped in with Randall several months ago. It had already been dusky when they'd arrived, and thanks to the cats, they hadn't stayed long.

He went to the back porch where he found a tarnished key beneath a wilted pot of geraniums. He dumped his bags on the porch steps and let himself inside, where he immediately started to sniffle and then sneeze. He'd taken allergy meds early this morning, but clearly they had worn off. He could smell the musty aroma of cats, but didn't see any, and without looking around—and hoping that perhaps they had all been carted off to some shelter—he held his breath as he opened the kitchen cupboard where Gram kept spare keys. Finding the set for the Pontiac, he hurried back outside, gasping to get a breath of fresh air.

But it was too late. As he went over to the small unattached garage, his eyes were already watering and his sneezing was getting louder. So much for his plan to change clothes at

Gram's house. He had no intention of remaining in that house for one moment longer than necessary.

"*Garrison?* Is that *you*?"

He paused from going into the garage. *"Ruby?"* He peered at the short, rounded woman. Her hair had turned snowy white, but her skin was still the color of an old copper penny and not nearly as wrinkled as he would've imagined.

"Land sakes!" she declared as she hurried over. "I heard all that sneezing and I thought it must be you." She threw her arms around him. "Welcome home, boy."

"Thank you, Ruby." He erupted into a new seizure of sneezing.

"You still have those allergies?"

"The cats"—he sneezed loudly—"triggered it." He reached into the pocket of his backpack for his allergy pills. "I need to take one of these."

"You need some water to wash it down?"

"Ye-yes." He sneezed again. "Please!"

"Come on." She tugged on his arm. "Let's get you inside where it's warm."

He didn't protest as she led him to her house, which was similar to Gram's only smaller. And it was still painted a cheerful yellow with white trim. "How have you been, Ruby?"

"Well, it was a blow to lose Lilly. Can't deny that. And you know my William passed on last spring." She opened the door, tugging him into her cozy kitchen where she quickly filled a glass of water and handed it to him. "Ain't easy gettin' old."

"I'm sorry about William." He popped a pill into his mouth and gulped the water.

"Thank you. I'm real sorry for your loss too, Garrison. Lilly was a fine woman." She pulled out a kitchen stool with a cracked plastic seat and pointed at him as if she expected him to sit.

He eased himself onto the stool, still sniffling.

"You want something else. Something to eat?"

"Sounds good, but I should probably be on my way soon."

"How 'bout some apple juice? Or a nice hot cup of tea? Cocoa?"

"You have cocoa?"

"Just the instant kind, but I—"

"That sounds perfect, Ruby. Walking from the bus stop made me feel chilled to the bone. I'm still not used to this climate. Uganda was so much warmer."

"And I know you got malaria while you were over there." She grimly shook her head as she turned the gas on beneath a cherry-red teakettle. "Thought you'd know better than that, young man. Lilly told me all about it. How you forgot to take your malaria medication and got yourself sicker than a dog." She made a tsking sound in her teeth. "Shame on you, Garrison."

Feeling like he was twelve again, he stared down at her plastic topped countertop—same old yellow-and-green daisies, only now it looked retro—straight out of the sixties, and it took him straight back to his childhood. "I know," he confessed. "I was really diligent about taking the antimalarial meds at first. But time went by . . . things got busy . . . I suppose I got a little careless. Unfortunately the chances of contracting malaria increase. The longer you stay in the country the more likely you are to contract it."

She patted him on the back. "Well, never mind that. I shouldn't have chided you for it. What you did over there in Uganda—that was *angels'* work, Garrison. God bless you for doing it. Lilly was real proud of you too. How many wells did you dig over there anyway?"

"A lot of people helped with the digging, Ruby."

"Oh, I know that, boy. But you were the brains. I know how you managed to work with the government and plan for the digging and everything. So how many you think you got put in?"

He shrugged as he unzipped his jacket. "Truth is, I sort of lost count after thirty."

She slowly shook her head. "To think that all those villages got good clean water thanks to you, Garrison."

He grinned. "And thanks to you too, Ruby. I happen to know that you faithfully sent money to the project. Just like Gram and lots of other generous supporters. We never could've done what we did without all that financial support. Takes a team to make a well."

"Not to mention our prayers," she reminded him. "That must've helped too."

He nodded.

"So what'll you do with yourself now that you're home?" She turned to the whistling kettle. "Any big plans?"

He pressed his lips together, wondering how much to divulge to Ruby. Then he remembered that she was Gram's best friend and confidante. And he had fully intended to tell Gram about his most recent dream. Why not tell Ruby? "Well . . . you know what I really want to do?" he said slowly. "Something I haven't told anyone . . . yet."

Her eyes lit up as she stirred the hot water into the cocoa powder. "What is it, Garrison? I'd just love to hear about it." She set the steaming cup in front of him.

"I know I can't make this dream happen right away." He

paused to take a sip. "I realize I'll need to raise some funds first. But I'd really like to make a halfway house for young men."

"A halfway house?" She looked curious. "What is that?"

"A place for guys to get better," he explained. "You see, a friend of mine in Uganda told me about his younger brother Jacob. This poor kid really struggled with addiction in his teens. When he was twenty he completed a thirty-day treatment program, but he just couldn't seem to get his feet solidly under him. Jacob eventually fell back into his old ways . . . died of an overdose just last year. My friend was devastated."

"Oh my." She paused from dipping a tea bag in her own cup. "How tragic."

"Yeah. And, even though I haven't had an addiction problem myself, I can relate to feeling disconnected. Being forced to give up Uganda . . . not having a job or a home to speak of . . . well, I can kind of understand how discouraged a young man might get. I get how he might want a place to call home . . . a way to connect with others."

"That sounds like a good dream, Garrison. I hope you get to build your halfway house. I'm going to put it on my prayer list."

"I plan to call it Jacob's House," he confided.

"Good, solid name. And I can just imagine it, Garrison. A homey place where a young man can get free from his old drug connections." Her dark eyes grew sad. "My grandson Elliott could use a place like that."

"Really?" Garrison remembered when Ruby's daughter Saundra used to bring her little boy to visit with Ruby. "How old is he now?"

"Twenty-four . . . going on fourteen."

Garrison nodded sadly. "Too bad."

"The poor boy has had some real struggles." She took a sip of tea. "Don't like to dwell on it too much. Better to just pray instead. Maybe the good Lord knows how to fix Elliott. Because I sure don't." She looked hopefully at Garrison. "But maybe you'll build something that can help—Jacob's House. I like the sound of it."

"Well, it's just a dream at this stage . . . but God willing . . . who knows?"

"Maybe you could use Lilly's house," she suggested eagerly. "It's got those four bedrooms."

He sighed. "That would be nice, but Gram had a reverse mortgage on it. She did that to pay for my college tuition and to make ends meet. I had always hoped to pay her back by now, but then I went to Uganda instead. Not exactly a get-rich-quick scheme. I'm sure that all her equity is gone by now."

"Yes, well, don't feel bad about that. Putting you through college and seeing you going off to Africa to help folks there—that was *exactly* what Lilly wanted for you. And you know what she believed, Garrison, *the good Lord will provide*. She never worried one minute about money. You shouldn't either."

He forced a smile. For the most part, he agreed with Ruby. But sometimes that "not worrying" thing was easier said than done. As he finished his cocoa, he asked if he could use her bathroom. "I'd like to freshen up and change my clothes before I go to see Gram's lawyer. I'd do it at Gram's . . . but those cats."

"Of course. You just make yourself at home, Garrison. There are no cats in this house." She frowned. "But I've been growing quite attached to Viola."

"Viola?"

"One of Lilly's cats." Her eyes lit up. "She's a big, beautiful gray cat with the softest coat of fur. I think Lilly said she is a Russian Blue, and I've always admired her. I think she's about twelve years old. My William never wanted a cat in the house. But now that he's gone . . ." She sighed. "Anyway, if you need to find homes for those cats, I'd like to be the first in line for Viola."

"Yes, of course," he eagerly agreed. "I don't see any reason you couldn't have her. For all I care, you can have all of the cats, Ruby."

She chuckled. "No sirree. Thank you very much. I used to take care of them for Lilly when she was gone. Not that she was gone much—that many cats tie a body down. Believe you me, I know how much work they can be. Lilly might've liked a houseful of cats, but it's not for me. Besides that, I couldn't afford all the cat food or vet bills. I probably can't afford to take in Viola." Her smile faded a little. "But I sure would enjoy having her for company."

"Well, as far as I'm concerned, Viola is all yours, Ruby."

Garrison felt a bit more presentable by the time he walked into the law office at two. Mr. Miller firmly shook his hand and once again expressed his sympathy. "Have a seat," he said, and waved to a black leather chair across from his sleek desk.

"Thanks for taking time to meet with me," Garrison said as he sat. "I doubt there's much estate to deal with, but I want to do things right. And I'm aware that my grandmother had a reverse mortgage on her home. I assume what little equity she had has been eaten up with taxes by now. And besides her old car, which needs some work, and a few household goods, I doubt there is much to discuss."

Mr. Miller didn't respond to this as he opened a large file folder.

"Oh . . ." Garrison cringed. "Unless she had debts. I hadn't really considered that, but I suppose it's likely. I know my college tuition was costly. And she helped support me in Uganda. I hope she didn't incur debt as a result. Although I will pay it all back if she did. I mean, I'm currently unemployed, but as soon as I get a—"

"No, no, don't worry. Your grandmother had no debt, Garrison." Mr. Miller looked across his desk. "In fact, she paid back her reverse mortgage about seven years ago."

"What?" Garrison was shocked. "How on earth did she manage to do that? She had nothing beyond some skimpy Social Security. You're probably aware that my grandparents were missionaries. I know for a fact that my grandmother lived as frugally as a church mouse."

"That might be so," Mr. Miller said. "But she had money."

Garrison frowned. "How is that possible?"

"Did Mrs. Brown tell you much about her parents?"

He tried to remember. "Well, she mentioned that they were opposed to her marriage to my grandfather. They thought she was throwing her life away to become a missionary. So they were kind of estranged. That's about all I know."

"Apparently her parents were fairly well off. Your grandmother's father was involved in the early days of the airline industry. He passed away about twenty years ago, leaving everything to his second wife. Then she passed away while you were overseas. According to your great-grandfather's will, the remains of his estate went to your grandmother."

Garrison was trying to absorb this. "So Gram *wasn't* poor? She was rich?"

"She wasn't a millionaire. And, as you mentioned, she continued to live quite frugally. I suspect she was comfortable with her lifestyle." Mr. Miller held up what looked like a bank statement. "The most money she ever spent was in donations—primarily to the Uganda Water Project. Her records show that she sent in a generous check every single month since inheriting the money."

"The Uganda Water Project?" He studied Mr. Miller. "That was the mission group that I worked with. I know she donated to it. But I never thought she could afford to give very much."

"Well, according to this, her support was significant. It appears that her checks were funneled through the church, but it was definitely designated to the water project. Your grandmother obviously believed in it. She's even left a nice endowment for the project."

"Wow . . ." He slowly shook his head, trying to absorb this. "I had no idea."

Mr. Miller flipped through some papers. "I'd like to go over the details of her will, Garrison. It is, well, shall I say a bit unconventional."

"Okay." Garrison leaned forward to listen.

"As you know, Lilly was very fond of her cats. But she was also well aware that you have severe cat allergies. She knew that she couldn't expect you to take care of them after she was gone. So she has asked you to take guardianship of the cats until you can find them each a good home."

"Oh?" He nodded. "That shouldn't be hard. In fact, I think I already found one home already."

"Not so fast." Mr. Miller held up a page. "There are some very specific stipulations for the placement of the cats."

"Oh . . . okay. What kind of stipulations?"

"Your grandmother made a list. Naturally, I'll give you a copy of all this, but I did promise your grandmother that I'd go over the whole thing with you. She suspected you'd be a bit surprised. She wanted to be certain that you thoroughly understood and accepted her plans."

"That's fine. Go ahead."

Mr. Miller cleared his throat. "First of all, the cats can only be placed in approved families. Second, the adoptive families must live in Mrs. Brown's neighborhood."

"That sounds doable."

"And the adoptive families must have resided in that neighborhood for at least a year. Mrs. Brown wants to be assured they're not transient. And the homes must be approved. Meaning that they are clean and safe for pets. She's made another checklist for this."

"Seriously?" Garrison shook his head. "It sounds more like finding homes for children than for cats."

"Her cats were her children."

"Well . . . yeah . . . I know."

"Do you want to hear the rest?"

"Of course." Garrison leaned back.

"The adoptive homes must have at least one person in the house for the better part of the day so that the cats aren't left alone for long periods of time. And if the cats are placed with married couples, the marriage needs to be stable and solid."

Garrison frowned. "How am I supposed to know—"

"Mrs. Brown has a list for that too." Mr. Miller peered

over the top of the paper. "It's all in a packet for you. Shall I continue?"

Garrison just nodded.

"If the adoptive homes qualify, the cats will be placed for a two-week trial period. After that, the guardian of the cats will conduct one surprise visit to ensure that the cats are happily settled into their new homes. If anything is amiss, the cats shall be removed. Then, after the cat has spent three weeks in the adoptive home, the cat guardian shall return and—"

"Is it just me, or does this all sound a little crazy?" Had Gram been getting senile? She sounded so sensible on the phone . . . but maybe he'd missed something.

"As I told you, Garrison, it is a little unconventional. That's why I'm going over some of the details now."

"But I don't get it. I mean, how will I ever find people like this? Seriously, who in their right mind would ever agree to jump all these hurdles—surprise visits and home inspections and all that—just to adopt some old lady's cat?"

"I'm aware that most people would be put off by these things."

"Then why did Gram insist on all this?"

"Because she wanted to be certain that all her beloved cats would be well cared for after she was gone."

"But it feels like you're asking me to do the impossible." Garrison ran his fingers through his hair. "I mean, after all, they are just cats."

"Are you saying that you do not wish to be the guardian of the cats?"

"No . . . I'm not saying that. It just sounds extremely complicated and difficult."

"Well, there is one little surprise that will make it a bit

easier." Mr. Miller laid down the papers. "All the adoptive families will be given a check for ten thousand dollars after you have determined that all six cats are settled and happy."

"Ten thousand dollars for adopting a cat?"

He just nodded.

"That's sixty thousand dollars total!"

"That's correct."

Garrison let out a low whistle. Was this for real?

"So you need to decide, Garrison. Do you want to agree to this responsibility? It was your grandmother's last wishes that you do this for her. But she knew about your allergies and she realized you might refuse—"

"I'll do it," he said suddenly. "It was obviously important to her. How could I not do it?"

Mr. Miller smiled. "She would be happy to know this."

"So am I supposed to tell these adoptive families that they'll get ten grand just for taking in a cat? I mean, that would make it pretty easy to find homes. Just run an ad in the newspaper or online and I'll bet my phone would start ringing nonstop."

"You could do it that way." Mr. Miller frowned as he slid some paperwork into a large manila envelope. "But that would make it difficult to sift the suitable adoptive homes from the gold diggers."

Garrison nodded. "Good point."

"Basically, it's up to you—I mean, how you choose to handle this. Your grandmother's final wish was for her cats to find good homes and for the people who adopted them to be blessed in the process. She was well aware that some of her cats were older and might not be easily placed. The last thing she wanted was for them to go to a pet shelter or wind up on the streets or be euthanized."

"That's understandable."

"And she realized that it would take you some time to work out the details of her final wishes," he continued. "To that end, she's left you some living expenses. Enough for a month or two, depending on how you handle it." He slipped what looked like a cashier's check into the envelope.

"That was thoughtful." Garrison knew that his tone sounded flat and unenthusiastic, but it was the best he could muster. It wasn't easy discovering that one's grandmother was fonder of her cats than her own grandson. He knew that was selfish on his part, but Gram knew he had allergies when she started taking in felines.

"She also put details about the cats in here." Mr. Miller grinned. "Complete dossiers with photos and vet records and everything she thought might be needed in the case of her demise."

"Seems she thought of everything." Garrison felt slightly overwhelmed. Was he really about to become the keeper of the cats?

"I expect you'll want to remain in your grandmother's house while you're acting as guardian and handling the placement of the cats."

Garrison shook his head. "Not with my allergies."

"Right." Mr. Miller closed the thick envelope and slid it across his desk toward Garrison. "I'll admit that Mrs. Brown's plan seemed a bit eccentric to me at first, but the more I spoke with her, the more I realized that her heart was in the right place. She really loved her cats."

Garrison let out a long sigh. "Yeah . . . that seems obvious." He hated to think he envied a bunch of aging cats, but he couldn't help himself. Gram's estate was going directly to the felines. And really, why shouldn't she disperse her money as she saw fit? After all, those cats had been a bigger part of her life than Garrison . . . at least for the past sixteen years. In reality, Garrison had spent only six years under her roof. It was clear, those cats were her family.

As Garrison drove home, he was determined to carry out Gram's last wishes to the best of his ability—and as quickly as possible. For starters, he would give Viola to Ruby. Surely that would make Gram happy. As he pulled into the driveway, he checked his watch to see that he still had a couple of hours on his allergy medicine. Besides that precaution, he had stopped by the drugstore to pick up a pack of disposable allergy masks as well as some medical-grade disposable gloves. He knew this might be overkill, but he didn't care. If necessary, he would get a respirator and maybe even a hazmat suit too. One couldn't be too careful.

"How'd it go with the lawyer?" Ruby asked. She'd emerged from her house just as he was closing the garage door.

He weighed his words. "It was . . . uh . . . interesting."

"Oh." She frowned.

"Do you still want Viola?"

Her eyes brightened. "Oh yes, I'd love to have her."

"Well, I need to find homes for *all* the cats. As soon as possible. It'd be great if you could take Viola off my hands and—"

"You won't have to ask me twice." Ruby followed him to the back door. "Do you think she'll be happy at my house?"

"I'm sure she'll be most grateful." He unlocked the door.

"I don't have any cat goodies . . . like food dishes and litter boxes."

"I'm sure Gram had plenty of that sort of thing." He paused to secure the mask and pulled on the gloves.

"You look like you're about to perform surgery," she commented as they went inside.

"Well, I do plan to remove some cats," he joked. "But not surgically."

She pushed ahead of him, calling out for Viola. "Here, kitty-kitty," she cooed sweetly. And just like that a small herd of cats came rushing into the kitchen. "They probably think I'm going to feed them again," she explained as she bent down to scoop up the big Russian Blue. "There you are, Viola girl. You wanna go home with Ruby?"

Garrison froze in place as the cats swarmed around his feet. He didn't want to show how unsettling this was, but he could feel his heart racing and it was getting difficult to breathe. Or maybe that was the mask. "Go ahead and look around for what you need," he told Ruby. "Cat food or dishes or whatever. Take anything you like."

"Are you okay?" She peered curiously at him. "Even for a white boy, you look awful pale. Are you having a malaria attack?"

"No, no . . . it's—uh—just the allergy thing," he murmured.

"Looks like more than that to me." She tilted her head to one side as she rubbed the top of Viola's head, studying him closely.

"More than what?" He carefully stepped over a big furry cat that resembled a raccoon.

"Looks to me like you might have some kind of phobia, boy."

"Phobia—of what?"

"Cats." She pushed Viola up close to his face and he quickly jumped back, accidentally stepping on a cat tail or paw and causing one of the felines to let out a loud screech that made him jump even higher. Ruby laughed loudly. "I do believe I'm right. You have a cat phobia, Garrison."

"No, no . . ." He tried to calm himself. "It's just the allergies. I like to keep a safe distance from—"

"I saw it on a TV show not long ago. Maybe it was Dr. Phil. Anyway, they said the best way to conquer your fears was to face them head-on." She grinned wide, revealing a gold tooth. "I guess that's what you're doing right now."

"Right now, I'm going upstairs," he told her. "I want to see if there are any rooms that have been off-limits to the cats." Mostly he just needed a place to steady himself, a spot where he could close the door and catch his breath.

"Lilly always kept your room closed up tight," she called after him. "Hoping you'd come home to stay with her a while. It should be a cat-free zone." She chuckled. "Imagine a big strong-looking young man afraid of a pretty little kitty like you, Viola."

"*Imagine*," he muttered to himself as he scaled the stairs. He went down the hall and directly to his old room, quickly opening the door and stepping inside. Once again, he was pleasantly surprised to see that it looked exactly as he'd left it straight out of high school. It was like going into a comfortable time warp. Sure, the sports posters were curled at the edges and the plaid curtains and matching bedspread had faded some, but for the most part, nothing had changed. A little more at ease, he closed the door and leaned against it. Then he cautiously removed the face mask and, taking in a slow, deep breath, he felt himself beginning to relax.

Was Ruby right? Did he really have some kind of cat phobia? He peered at his image in the cloudy dresser mirror. His brow was furrowed and his hazel eyes looked worried, and even his pupils appeared smaller. Wasn't that a sign of fear? And yet, what did he have to be afraid of? He'd traveled the world, faced various forms of danger—everything from wild jungle animals to guerrilla warriors—and he had never felt unreasonably fearful of anything. And yet, it was undeniable, those silly old cats in the kitchen had just sent shivers down his spine. Maybe Ruby was right after all. It was possible that he was dealing with some kind of phobia. Perhaps he should take her advice (or the advice of that TV doctor she'd mentioned) and simply face his fears.

He looked around his old room, wondering if it might be possible to actually stay in Gram's house. It would certainly save him some hotel expenses. With this haven in his old room, he might be able to get by for a week or so. Hopefully it wouldn't take long to find homes for Gram's herd of felines. In the meantime, he'd attempt to take Ruby's advice by facing his fears and getting to know these cats better. At least he'd try.

"*Yoo-hoo?*" she called as she clumped up the stairs. "Are you okay, Garrison?"

He put his mask back on, adjusting it snugly against his

cheeks. It was one thing to face one's fears, something else altogether to expose oneself to disturbing allergens. "I'm coming," he called as he emerged from his room, carefully closing the door behind him.

"I found some cat supplies," she informed him. "Lilly had a whole closet just chock-full of kitty goodies. I helped myself, like you told me to—hope that's okay."

"It's more than okay," he assured her as they went down the stairs. "Anything to get you and Viola off to a good start in her new home." Bracing himself, he reached out to give the gray cat a quick rub on the head. Baby steps, he said to himself. One cat at a time. "I hope you two are very happy together," he told Ruby. "And, uh, well . . . I shouldn't say anything, Ruby, but my grandma has made some provisions for the, uh, for the folks that adopt her cats."

"Provisions?" Ruby's brows drew together. "What do you mean?"

"I don't really want to go into the details now. But if you and Viola settle in nicely and you decide you want to keep her—"

"I already *know* I want to keep her," Ruby declared. "No question about that."

"Well then you shouldn't worry too much about the expenses of cat food and litter and vet bills and such."

She gave him a puzzled look. "What're you talking about, boy?"

"Gram made some provisions for her cats' new homes."

"What do you mean *provisions*?" she asked again.

He made a mischievous grin. "I shouldn't have said anything."

"You got that right, young man. You tell Ruby something like that and then leave her hanging?"

He held up his purple-gloved hands. "I'm sorry, Ruby. But that's all I can say right now. Okay?"

"Hmm . . . I guess so." Her mouth twisted to one side. "Now, you better take care of yourself and your little cat phobia, young man. I set my cat things out on the back porch. I'd like to get Viola home now. And I'll be sure to let you know how she likes living at my place."

"Thanks," he told her as they went into the kitchen.

"You let me know if you need anything." She sounded like her old cheerful self again. "Or if these cats start a-worrying you, just give old Ruby a call. I'll come to your rescue."

"Thanks. Appreciate it."

"Or if you get hungry, you come on over. In fact, I've a mind to just whip up some chicken pot pie tonight." She gave him a sly look as she wrapped part of her coat over Viola. "Maybe I'll see if I can bribe you with food . . . get you to talk."

He chuckled. "Ruby, Ruby."

"Or maybe you don't like my pot pie like you used to?"

"I haven't had a good pot pie in years," he said eagerly.

"Alrighty then. My stomach don't like eating too late at night. Come five thirty, you get yourself over to Ruby's kitchen and don't you be late."

"Will do." He saluted her.

"And I assume you'll take over feeding the cats now."

"Yes, of course."

She pointed to the refrigerator where a laminated page was attached by a cat-shaped magnet. "That's Lilly's detailed instructions. She always kept it there for me. Sometimes if she had to be gone for a spell—never more'n a day at most—I'd see to the cats."

He glanced at the note. "Good to know." He opened the

door for her and seeing her box of cat goods, scooped them up and followed her over to her house.

"Thank you, son." She rewarded him with a wide smile.

"Thank you for taking Viola." He set the box on a chair inside her back door.

"See you at five thirty."

"You bet." He grinned to himself as he closed her door. *One cat gone, five to go*. Maybe this wasn't going to be so hard after all. And it warmed his heart to imagine Ruby's expression when he handed her a check for ten thousand dollars next month. By his calculations that should be a little before Christmas. *Nice!*

He retrieved the duffle bag he'd stashed in the Pontiac and carried it, along with the envelope from Mr. Miller, into the house. He wanted to read through the papers from Gram's attorney, but as soon as he got back into the kitchen, the cats began converging and meowing . . . as if they expected something from him. *What?* A glance at Gram's directions on the fridge revealed these cats were used to eating their dinner between four and five. And it was just a little past four.

Still wearing the particle mask and gloves, he removed Gram's instructions from the fridge and continued reading. He quickly realized this was more complicated than just filling a big bowl with Cat Chow. Each cat was listed individually. Even with Viola adopted by Ruby, there were still five different feline diets to contend with. Garrison had to read through it several times, condensing it down to this: Oreo had to be fed by himself in the laundry room with just a special low-fat dry food because he was overweight and would devour the other cats' foods if he got the chance; meanwhile, Spooky needed special drops in her canned food to prevent hairballs; Rusty had a special mix of both dry and canned food; and Muzzy needed to be fed a special gluten-free food. It seemed that the only cat without special dietary needs was Harry.

"God bless Harry," Garrison said as he laid the instruction sheet on the counter. Then he looked around at the cats clamoring around his feet. "Which one of you is Harry?"

The big raccoon-like cat seemed to look up expectantly, rubbing himself against Garrison's legs as if to confirm that he indeed was Harry. "Well, that's easy for you to say," Garrison told the friendly cat. "But I need more evidence." Now he remembered the "dossier" that Mr. Miller had described. Hadn't he mentioned photos?

He opened the envelope and dug through it until he found the section that described the cats. Seeing that it was rather lengthy, he decided to take it up to his room where he could read it without wearing his mask and gloves. "I'll be back soon," he promised the cats as he hurried away.

The top page was for Viola, but since she had already found a home, he barely skimmed it. However, he did discover that, besides being a Russian Blue, Viola was twelve years old and slightly moody. She was very attached to Gram and considered herself to be the top cat. "Viola will not do well in a house with children and noise or other pets," Gram had written. "She would prefer being re-homed with a mature single woman who is affectionate and can bestow on Viola the special attention that she craves."

Garrison chuckled. Well, Ruby should be just about perfect. Really, this wasn't so difficult. He sat down on his bed and flipped to the next page. A photo of a big orange short-haired cat grinned back at him. *Rusty.* Apparently this cat was ten years old, fairly easygoing, and got along with children. "Rusty is the clown cat," Gram had written. "He is playful and loving and would enjoy a home with a big family and lots of attention and even other cats. Rusty gets along well with others."

"Good old Rusty," Garrison said as he set that page aside.

Spooky, he soon discovered, was the calico, a seven-year-old female that Gram had taken in two years ago. She was also the least social of the cats and very moody. "Spooky is independent, but she still likes attention. She would probably do best in a home without other pets." Since he had three cats to go and he knew they were hungry, he didn't bother to read all the details about Spooky.

He saw the photo of the black-and-white cat. Naturally, that was Oreo. That was easy to remember. He was nine years old and had come to Gram as a kitten. He sounded easygoing enough.

The loud Siamese cat was Muzzy. She was eight years old and according to Gram, "somewhat demanding and talkative." Garrison set her page aside.

Finally he saw the page for Harry—and, as it turned out, he *was* the friendly cat that resembled a raccoon. Harry was a Maine Coon cat that had found his way into Gram's home and heart just a year ago. "Harry is a very special cat," she had written. "I don't like to say he's my favorite, but if I could only keep one cat—God forbid—I would choose Harry. He is five years old and the smartest one of the bunch."

Armed with this new information, Garrison put on his particle mask again and went down to the kitchen to feed the cats. Naturally, it wasn't as easy as he thought it should be, but eventually he got the cats figured out and situated and fed. By the time he finished up it was nearly five—and he felt exhausted.

Not only that, but his nose was starting to run and his eyes were watering and by the time he made it to his room, he was starting to sneeze again. How could caring for five felines be this difficult? And, seriously, if he couldn't manage a few silly old cats, how did he ever think he could run a halfway house for recovering addicts?

4

I think what you're saying is that Lilly created some kind of endowment fund for her beloved kitties," Ruby said as she gave him a second helping of chicken pot pie.

"I said nothing of the sort." He kept his eyes fixed on his plate.

"You might not-a said the words." She sat back down. "But I can tell that's what you mean." She reached over and put her hand over his. "You can trust me, Garrison."

He looked up and grinned. "Well, you probably know that Gram was always a generous woman."

She nodded as she picked up her fork. "Especially when it came to the cats." She chuckled as she dug into her second helping. "Generous to a fault."

After stuffing himself on the delicious pot pie, Garrison went back home and barricaded himself against the cats.

Stowed away up in his boyhood room, sitting at the desk that was a couple inches too short for him, he opened up his laptop and proceeded to write out an ad for the local classifieds. He also planned to place it on Craigslist and some other local sites. No stone unturned. The sooner he found homes for these cats, the better for all.

> Five very special cats have lost their owner and are looking for new homes. Take your pick: a Siamese named Muzzy, a short-haired black-and-white named Oreo, an orange tiger named Rusty, a calico named Spooky, or a Maine Coon cat named Harry. All are well mannered and between five and twelve years old. All cats are fixed and in good health. Vet records available. "Adoptive" parents must meet certain qualifications and live in northeast Vancouver. Call for more information.

He reread the ad, then typed in the phone numbers and his email address. Satisfied with it, he went ahead and posted it on the internet and emailed it to the newspaper. He also planned to make some signs to post in the neighborhood. Hopefully he would start getting inquiries by tomorrow.

Morning came and neither his cell phone nor Gram's landline was ringing. And so, after feeding the hungry horde of cats, Garrison set about creating what he felt would be an attractive and compelling poster. Protected by his allergy medicine and a fresh particle mask, he spent about an hour taking various photos of the cats. Then, safely back in his room, he selected a photo of Oreo and Rusty and, with the help of his laptop, put together a poster. He was just putting on the finishing touches when his phone rang. Hoping it was someone calling to adopt a cat, he eagerly answered. But it was Gram's pastor, calling to express his sympathy and finalize some details regarding the memorial service.

"We could have held it Saturday," Pastor Barton told him. "But the women are having their harvest fair tomorrow. They always have it the weekend before Thanksgiving."

"Monday is fine," Garrison assured him.

"Your grandmother was very specific about the kind of service she wished to have," he said. "And, as you know, she chose cremation. Her plan was to keep everything sweet and simple. She even wrote her own very humble eulogy. She didn't want anyone to make her sound overly grand. So, anyway, it's all rather cut-and-dried. Well, I don't mean to sound like that. She actually planned a very nice service. And she hoped that you would want to speak, Garrison. In fact, I'm sure the congregation would enjoy that too."

"Of course," he promised. "I'm glad to."

They discussed it a bit more before Garrison told the pastor he'd see him on Monday and hung up. He wasn't surprised that Gram had handled everything so efficiently. She had always been a practical, no-nonsense sort of woman—in life . . . and in death. Well, except for the cats. It seemed like she'd thrown practicality out the window when she'd started taking them in.

Her whole house, he'd discovered, seemed dedicated to her fine, furry friends. There were cat basket beds in every room. Not that the cats seemed to use them. Most of the furnishings were covered in hair. There were cat toys scattered about, sometimes making the house seem like a minefield—especially when he wasn't paying close attention. And some rather inventive scratching posts were stuck here and there. One reached clear to the ceiling with several platforms as well as a crow's nest on top. However, the upholstered furniture must've been preferable to the cats because everything was scratched and threadbare. Apparently the cats didn't understand the rationale of "scratching posts." Except for Harry. Garrison caught Harry working over the giant post with great vigor as he headed out to get his cat posters printed.

"Good kitty," he said as he passed through the living room. Harry turned and peered at Garrison with intelligent green eyes, almost as if he understood. "Take care of things while I'm gone," he told the cat.

After getting a bite to eat and some posters printed, Garrison returned to Gram's neighborhood and began putting them up here and there.

"What's this?" a young woman on a bicycle asked him.

He smiled at her. "Free cats," he said cheerfully. "You interested?"

She got off the bicycle and studied the poster. "As a matter of fact, I've wanted a cat for years. And I've been promising myself to get one ever since I got settled in a real house."

"Are you settled in a 'real' house now?" he asked in a teasing tone.

She nodded. "I am."

"Well, I have a nice selection of cats to choose from." He explained about his grandmother and how the felines had been her beloved family.

"Was your grandma the Cat Lady?" Her brows rose.

"I suppose some people called her that." He gave the nail head one last whack then turned back to the girl. With her dark brown ponytail and expressive brown eyes, she was strikingly pretty. "Did you know my grandmother—the, uh, Cat Lady?"

"No, but I heard she had a lot of cats. Like twenty?"

"As far as I know, she only had seven—at the most. Although I'll admit that's more than enough."

"Oh, well . . . you know how rumors go," she said apologetically. "This is a pretty tight-knit neighborhood. People talk."

"Yeah. Anyway, my grandmother passed on last week. It's up to me to find good homes for her cats."

"I'm sorry for your loss." She looked genuinely sympathetic.

"Thanks. I realize my grandmother was old and she was probably ready to go . . . but I still miss her."

"Well, if these cats are as nice as you say, I might be interested in giving one a home," she proclaimed. "But I'd like to meet the cats first."

"No problem." He frowned and pointed to a bullet on the sign. "But you have to live in this neighborhood." He made an uncomfortable smile. "My grandma has a whole list of requirements for potential adoptive homes."

"Well, that's no problem. I live just a few blocks from here."

"Perfect."

She stuck out her hand. "I'm Cara Wilson," she told him.

"Garrison Brown," he said as he clasped her warm hand. "Pleased to meet you."

"So is this a good time to see your cats?" she asked hopefully.

"Absolutely," he said eagerly.

"Great. I'm taking my break. Not that I'm really locked into a schedule. You see, I mostly work from home. Except for once a week when I have to go in for planning meetings."

"Well, there's no time like the present." He grimaced to remember the condition of the house. "Although I should warn you my grandmother's place is, well, a little catty . . . if you know what I mean."

She chuckled as she tucked a long strand of shiny chestnut hair behind one ear. "That's okay. I had a great-aunt who used to keep cats. I totally understand."

After Garrison told her the address, she said she'd drop her bike at home and drive her car over. "Just in case I get to bring the cat back home with me."

As he hurried back to Gram's, he felt greatly encouraged on two levels. First of all, he might've just found a home for another cat. That took the cat population down to four! But secondly, and probably even more significant, this girl had really caught his eye. Not only was Cara very pretty, in a wholesome girl-next-door sort of way, there was something else too. He couldn't quite put his finger on it—maybe it was a mixture of kindness and spunk—but he was certain he wanted to get better acquainted with her.

As soon as he reached Gram's house, he automatically pulled on the particle mask. He'd given up the surgical gloves, except for kitty litter cleaning, which he'd already done this morning. But despite his allergy meds, he knew the mask was a true necessity. Without it he was a mess. However, due to wanting to impress his visitor, he was tempted to shove it back into his pocket. Except the image of him sneezing and wheezing and coughing all over the poor girl was truly alarming. Really, which was less attractive—impersonating a surgeon or having an allergic fit?

As he kicked some cat toys under the sofa, he wished he'd taken the time to straighten up some. Gram's house really could use a thorough cleaning and he fully intended to do that . . . but getting rid of these cats was his first priority. After that, he planned to empty most of the contents of the house—at least the items that were coated in fur or had been shredded by claws. Even the wall-to-wall carpeting needed to be removed.

The doorbell rang and he hurried to open it. "Welcome to the cat house," he told her, grinning from behind his white mask as he waved her inside.

"What's that?" She pointed to his face.

"I have severe cat allergies," he explained.

She frowned. "That must be rough . . . I mean, with all these cats."

"It's definitely a challenge." As she went over to where Rusty and Oreo were playing together on the sofa, he quickly explained about how he'd been out of the country for nine years. "My grandmother helped raise me, but after I left home, she was lonely. So she started to collect cats."

She was stroking Oreo's sleek coat and scratching Rusty's head. "You two are so sweet," she said. "You look just like the picture on the poster."

He told her their names. "They're the friendliest of the cats." Just then Harry strolled into the living room, rubbing himself against Garrison's legs. "Well, I guess Harry is friendly too."

Cara looked over and her eyes lit up. "That's a Maine Coon cat," she exclaimed.

"Yeah, I know."

"Those are very special cats." She came over and kneeled down, running her fingers through Harry's long silky coat. "Oh, he is really a beauty."

"I've never been fond of cats," Garrison confessed, "but I have to admit he's a nice one. He was Gram's favorite too."

"Oh, he's perfectly lovely." Cara scooped the big cat into her arms, carrying him over to the sofa. "You are a darling," she cooed at him. Harry seemed to be eating up the attention. "And those pale green eyes. I can see real intelligence in them."

"Yes," Garrison agreed. "I think he's very smart."

"How old is he?"

"He's the youngest of the cats. Just five," Garrison explained. "But according to Gram's notes, Maine Coon cats sort of rule the cat kingdom. And I've noticed it too. It's like he has this regal quality about him."

"I adore him. Honestly, I think I'm in love." Cara looked up with glowing eyes. "Can I *really* have him?"

Suddenly Garrison remembered the stipulations of Gram's will. "I, uh, I think so. But I have to ask you some questions first." He made a sheepish smile. "It was my grandmother's dying wish that these cats get placed in the right homes."

"Sure. I can understand that."

"Well, I already know that you live in the neighborhood. And you work from home."

"Yes. I write for a relatively new online travel magazine. The pay's not so fabulous . . . not yet anyway. But the magazine has huge potential. And I've been with them for almost five years now. The longest I've been at any job."

"That's great." He tried to remember the list. "Are you married?"

She frowned. "I have to be married?"

"No," he said quickly. "But if you're married, Gram wanted to be assured you're in a solid marriage."

She chuckled. "Well, I am solidly single."

He grinned. "Maybe I should get the list, so we can go over it. This is still kind of new turf for me."

"Why don't you do that?" She turned back to Harry, cooing at him as she continued to stroke his coat. "You are a truly lovely creature, Harry. Would you like to go home with me? Be my cat? We could be very happy together."

Garrison hurried to the kitchen where he'd left the large envelope, quickly extracting Gram's long list of requirements. "Here it is," he said as he reappeared in the living room. "Okay . . . you live in the neighborhood." He peered over the page at her, taking in her profile, the upturned nose, firm chin. "Have you been here at least a year?"

She looked up with concern. "At least a year?"

He nodded. "That's a stipulation."

"Well, no . . . I've only been here since August."

He frowned. "What?"

"But it's not like I'm going to leave."

Garrison scanned the list, seeing something else that Gram's attorney hadn't specifically mentioned. "Do you own your home?"

"I have to own my home?" She sounded slightly indignant. "No . . . I'm renting."

"Oh . . ." Garrison stared at the line stating "adoptive owners must be homeowners in the neighborhood." Homeowners, really?

"So are you saying I don't qualify?"

He felt really torn. "According to this . . . you don't."

She gently removed Harry from her lap, setting him next to her on the sofa. "You mean just because I don't own my home—haven't lived here a year—you aren't going to let me have Harry?" She looked close to tears, and Garrison felt like a real jerk.

"I would gladly give you Harry," he said meekly. "But this list—it was given to me by the lawyer—it's my grandmother's dying wish."

Cara slowly stood. "Well, I wish you the best of luck in finding homes for your *five* cats," she said a bit stiffly.

"I'm really sorry," he said as he followed her to the front door. "If I could do it differently, I would. I mean, I'm as eager as you are—"

"I feel like I've been the victim of a bait and switch." Her eyes narrowed with suspicion. "Like I've been tricked."

"I didn't mean to trick you. It's just that I have to—"

"Don't worry, Garrison." Her smile looked forced. "I'll get over it." She turned around to give Harry one last glance. "Take care, big boy. I hope you find the right home."

"I'm really sorry, Cara, but I have to respect my—"

"Never mind," she said abruptly. "I get it." And then she left.

Garrison sneezed beneath the mask, causing it to slip off his face. And now his eyes were watering up. He could tell his allergy meds were wearing off. Harry sauntered over and rubbed up against his legs, letting out a friendly meow.

"It's not your fault, old boy." Garrison sneezed again. "Man, I gotta get outta here."

By the morning of the memorial service on Monday, Garrison had not managed to find a home for a single cat. He'd gotten only one phone call and that was from a woman who lived downtown. But at least he'd learned something. Rule number one: go over the basic stipulations before talking about the available cats.

However, cats were the last thing on his mind as he drove to the church. First and foremost, his thoughts were with Gram, and he knew this service had been important to her. Even though she'd written her own eulogy, he knew it was only respectful to say a few words. He also knew that public speaking was not his forte. The truth was, he'd rather get a root canal than address a roomful of people. Although his jacket pocket bulged from the numerous index cards he'd scribbled on last night, he hoped he wouldn't need to pull them out and fumble through them. But whatever it took, he was determined to honor Gram's memory today.

"My grandmother took me in after my parents died," Garrison began when it was his turn to speak. "I didn't want to admit it at the time, since I was nearly twelve years old, but I was a little afraid of her when I first moved into her house. Or maybe I was just in awe of her. I'd grown up hearing my dad speak of his parents with a mixture of pride and almost fearful respect. I knew my grandparents were missionaries in Kenya. I knew that they'd lived through a lot of tough challenges. I'm sorry to say that I probably challenged Gram as much or more than her beloved villagers, the ones she was forced to leave behind when my grandfather died. But Gram never gave up on me. She was the first person in my life to teach me what real unconditional love was like. I will always be grateful to her for that." He sighed as he gazed over the nearly full sanctuary. Gram had more friends than he had realized.

"Gram taught me a lot of valuable things. Like telling the truth and persevering even when a situation looked like it was hopeless. She helped me to see the world as a bigger place than just what's within our borders. She taught me to have compassion for the less fortunate. Because of her I served in Uganda for nine years. Nine years that have changed my life forever—and have helped mold me into the person I am today. I feel like I owe all that to my grandmother. Without her influence on my life, I cannot imagine where I would be today." *Well, aside from being the caretaker for a houseful of cats*, he thought a bit grimly, but naturally, he didn't say this.

Instead he finished by telling a story about how Gram had discovered he'd stolen some tokens from a video arcade and how she'd made him go take them back and confess to the owner. "I was so ashamed," he told them. "But when we got home my grandmother simply opened her Bible and read a verse about Jesus forgiving someone. I can't even remember which verse it was. But Gram looked at me and said, 'It's no different with you. Confess your sins to our Lord and he will forgive you your sins. That's all there is to it.'" He smiled. "I have taken those words with me wherever I've gone. I always will."

After the service, he visited with old friends from the church. They seemed genuinely happy to see him, and Gram's good friend Mrs. Spangle even invited him to come and speak to their missions group. He gave her his phone number and promised to make himself available.

"And is there anything I can do for you?" she asked.

"If you know anyone who wants to adopt a cat," he said quickly. "Someone who lives in my grandmother's neighborhood."

"I do know of a good no-kill animal shelter. Perhaps you could—"

"No, no. It's my grandmother's last wish that I make sure they find good homes."

Her thin brows arched. "Oh, my. Well, I wish you luck with that. Last I heard there was an abundance of cats in the Northwest."

As Garrison drove home, he wondered if it was time to revamp his feline relocation plan. The attorney had discouraged him from letting the word out about the monetary reward that would go to adoptive homes. But perhaps he could drop some subtle hints in a revised classified ad. Sweeten the deal, so to speak.

The morning after Gram's memorial service, Garrison called Mr. Miller. "I have some questions I hadn't considered when I spoke to you last week," he told him.

"Yes, I expected you would. Any luck finding homes for the cats?"

"I placed one right next door." Then he explained about his ads and posters and how he'd almost found a home for another cat. "But the woman didn't fit Gram's criteria. She'd only lived in the neighborhood a few months. But she seemed like a good choice, I wish I could've given—"

"Sorry, Garrison. My job is to respect your grandmother's final wishes. I'm sure you can understand that."

"Yes, well, that's not really why I called. Mostly I wanted to know what's to become of my grandmother's house. I know she'd had that reverse mortgage on it. But since I'm kind of stuck here for a while—I mean, until I get the cats resettled—I hoped I could empty it out a little. Also, there are some family things I'd like to keep if that's all right."

"It's all yours, Garrison. Other than what your grandmother set aside for the cats, the remaining estate is yours. However, you won't officially inherit it until you get the cats successfully placed in new homes. It's all spelled out in the packet I gave you."

"Oh . . . yeah . . . I haven't read through the whole thing yet."

"So feel free to do as you like with the house. As I mentioned in my office, your grandmother paid off the reverse mortgage. The house is free and clear."

"Free and clear?"

"Absolutely. I have the title on file here. When your task is finished, it will be signed over to you."

"So this is *my* house?" Garrison looked around the cluttered and run-down kitchen with wonder as reality set in.

"It will be. When the cats are re-homed."

"Right." Garrison considered this. "That's really great. Thanks!"

"Thank your grandmother."

"Yeah, of course."

When Garrison hung up, he walked through the somewhat shabby four-bedroom house, taking it all in and suddenly seeing it with a fresh set of eyes. This place had real potential. If he fixed it up and sold it, he might get enough capital to start the halfway house he'd been dreaming of creating. He closed his eyes and sent a silent thank-you to his grandmother. She really hadn't forgotten him. Not at all.

For the rest of the day, Garrison threw himself into cleaning, sorting, repairing, and disposing. It was good therapy, and the results were making themselves visible by Wednesday.

"My goodness!" Ruby exclaimed when she came in to see what was happening. "I hardly recognize the place. What's going on?"

"It started with removing some of the furnishings that were beyond hope," he confessed.

"Yes, I saw the mess in the front yard."

"Sorry about that. I've got someone coming to pick them up on Friday." He adjusted his particle mask, wiping a streak of sweat from his upper lip. "After that I just kept going. One thing led to another." He glanced around the somewhat vacant living room. Other than the scratching posts and a couple pieces of furniture, the place looked stark. "I'm afraid I've upset some of the cats." He nodded to an old chair where Rusty and Oreo were nestled together. "I hauled this piece back inside so they'd have something familiar."

Ruby pointed over to where Spooky was sitting on the stairway, looking at them through the banister with what seemed a disgruntled expression. "That one does not look happy."

He shook his head. "Yeah. Spooky is pretty mad at me. And Muzzy has been very loudly expressing herself too. Harry's the only one who seems to still like me." He made a sheepish grin. "But I figure I'm doing them all a favor . . . making it easier for them to go."

"Any responses to your ads?"

"A couple of calls, but the people didn't fit Gram's criteria."

"Too bad. Viola is settling in very nicely at my place. She doesn't even seem to miss the other cats."

"Good to know." He considered mentioning the bonus Ruby would receive in a few weeks. "Any interest in taking on a second cat?"

"Oh, no. Viola is plenty of cat for me. And I do believe

she's happier having me all to herself." Ruby chuckled. "She's already decided that my bed is her bed and truth be told, I don't mind a bit."

"That's great. Well, I guess I should write up another ad for the cats. Maybe I can put some kind of Christmas spin on it. *Give your loved one a cat for Christmas*?"

Ruby looked uncertain. "Speaking of Christmas, I came over to invite you to Thanksgiving dinner tomorrow. Some single folks in the neighborhood are getting together to share potluck."

"Right, I almost forgot about Thanksgiving. That sounds great. What can I bring?"

"Nothing." She waved her hand. "I just saw the condition of your kitchen. Doesn't look like any real cooking is gonna happen in there."

"I'm getting ready to paint in there. But I could pick something up at the—"

"Never you mind. These old gals are already cooking up a storm."

"If they cook half as good as you, it should be delicious."

"Dinner is at two," she said as she was leaving. "You can drive us."

"It's not at your house?"

"No. But I have directions. We'll leave a little before two."

After working all Thursday morning, Garrison showered and shaved and dressed in his favorite black pullover sweater and tan cords. As he pulled on his jacket, he felt Harry rubbing himself against his legs. Realizing that he'd forgotten to put on a fresh particle mask after shaving, Garrison was surprised that he wasn't having another sneezing fit. Maybe his allergy meds were working better these days. Or maybe he was building some resistance. He bent down and scratched Harry's head. "You're a good old boy," he told him. "More like a dog than a cat."

Harry seemed to nod, almost as if he understood and agreed.

"Take care of things, buddy. I'll be back in a few hours." He chuckled. "I'm off to dine with—a bunch of old ladies."

Ruby directed Garrison several blocks away. "There, that's it. The little brown house with the gingerbread trim. Inviting, isn't it?"

"Unless there's a wicked witch living inside." He chuckled as he parked across the street.

Ruby snickered. "I don't think our hostess would appreciate that comment."

He carried Ruby's heavy basket of food, following her up the narrow brick walkway. "Lots of cars out here," he said as she rang the bell. "This house looks a little small. Think we'll all fit?"

"Cara insisted on having it here. It's the first time she's lived in a real house and she really wanted to host this gathering."

"Cara?" He suddenly remembered the pretty brown-haired girl on the bike. "Is this Cara, uh, elderly?"

Ruby laughed. "Not in the least."

He felt his face flushing as Cara opened the door. Wearing a garnet-colored knit dress and with her dark hair pinned up, she looked even prettier than he remembered. Suddenly he wished he'd thought to bring a hostess gift. Like a cat.

"Come in." She blinked in surprise as she opened the door wider.

Ruby started an introduction, but Cara stopped her. "Garrison and I have already met." She made a forced smile. "He refused to part with one of his precious cats."

Ruby frowned at him. "Oh . . . but Cara would make a wonderful pet owner. I would vouch for her. I've known her aunt for ages and—"

"Speaking of that, Aunt Myrtle is in the kitchen." Cara took their coats. "She and Gladys have taken over and I think they'd appreciate your help, Ruby. They both agree that you make the best gravy." Cara led Ruby back through the somewhat crowded house. Left to his own, Garrison proceeded to introduce himself to some of the other guests. Although a few were younger, most of them seemed to be closer to his grandmother's age. Before long, he found himself cornered by a pair of elderly sisters who had been good friends with Gram. Naturally, they wanted to hear all about him and what he'd been doing the past couple of decades.

After answering the Dorchester sisters' questions about Uganda and explaining how he'd contracted malaria, he used the opportunity to tell them about Gram's cats. "I'm looking for good homes," he told them. "Can I interest you ladies in adopting a cat or two?"

The older sister wrinkled her nose. "I'm sorry, Garrison, but I don't care much for cats."

"That's right," her sister agreed. "Winifred had a bad experience as a child. She abhors cats."

"To be honest, I'm not terribly fond of cats myself, but I'm trying to adapt to them. I tell myself it's mind over matter. I hope that if I don't think about it too much, it won't matter." He chuckled and then explained about his allergies. "If I forget to take my antihistamines I am a complete mess."

"You should eat ginger," the older sister said. "It helps with my hay fever."

"Really?" Garrison nodded at them as he glanced over to where Cara was welcoming an older man into her home, hugging him and taking his coat. The perfect hostess . . . to everyone else.

Garrison put great effort into acting natural and relaxed as he chatted and dined with his neighbors, but the whole while he felt uneasy. Plus he was distracted with keeping one eye on the pretty hostess. Partly because he couldn't help himself, and partly because he sensed that Cara was purposely avoiding him. She was never rude, but at the same time she never exchanged more than the briefest of conversation with him. Yet she remained friendly and warm and congenial to everyone else. It was unnerving.

For that reason, Garrison made an excuse to leave early—even before dessert was served. He knew it was bad manners as he abruptly thanked his hostess, but it was the best he could do under the circumstances. After being reassured that Ruby could get a ride home, he explained his need to see to his cats. Naturally, this led to some goodhearted teasing at his expense. Particularly from some of the younger guests that, due to the Dorchester sisters, he'd not had the opportunity to get acquainted with.

He forced a smile, waved goodbye, and tried to take the whole social fiasco in stride as he left. So what if they shared some laughs at his expense after he was gone. He was just relieved to get away from there. Not only had that "charming" little gingerbread house been overly small and overly crowded, it had literally felt as if the walls had been closing in on him.

As he drove home, he thought about Cara. She had looked so pretty in that deep-red dress. And she had such an engaging smile. An endearing laugh. Yet it was obvious that the girl was harboring a serious grudge against him. She must've taken it personally when he'd refused to hand over Harry. He wished he could explain the will dilemma to her again—to somehow make her understand—but really, what more could he say? Perhaps it was best to let sleeping dogs lie . . . or should he say *sleeping cats*?

6

Garrison knew that his heart was softening toward Gram's small herd of cats. Okay, he didn't actually like *all of* them. Muzzy's obnoxious Siamese howling was truly disturbing and Spooky's moodiness was irritating, but he attributed their bad manners to their general displeasure with him . . . and missing their previous owner. However, Rusty and Oreo were fairly easy to get along with. And then there was Harry . . . that big, slightly wild-looking animal had the best feline manners, not to mention intelligence. Harry was clearly his favorite. Even so Garrison knew he needed to find homes for all five of them. Good homes. No regrets.

This was driven even more firmly home when his phone rang on Friday morning. The man who had interviewed him last week, the same day that Gram had died, was calling to offer him the job. Garrison explained about his grandmother. "So I really need to see to some things regarding her estate," he told him. "I might be able to tie it up in a week. Maybe two if I'm lucky."

"No problem. December is always a slow month for the foundation. Although I would like to get you in the office for some important meetings before Christmas." He listed some specific dates. "That's when we start planning for the upcoming year. We have a big fundraiser in February and I like getting tasks pinned down before Christmas. Makes January go smoother."

"I'm sure I can wrap this up in two weeks max," Garrison assured him. "I'll be there in time for those planning meetings. Thank you, sir."

"I look forward to working with you, son. I really liked your résumé and that you'd spent that much time in Uganda. I can tell you're a diligent young man, and that you take your responsibilities seriously and see things through. I know you'll be a real asset to the team, Garrison."

In the spirit of diligence, Garrison started constructing a new ad on Friday afternoon. It was obvious that his first ad had been ineffective. For the new ad, Garrison decided to lure interest by mentioning that the cats would come with a special "Christmas bonus." He was careful not to mention cash, but he did word it in a mysterious way that he hoped would garner some prospective pet owners' curiosity.

He was just editing the ad when the phone rang. "Hey, Garrison," a woman's voice said. "I heard you're looking for homes for your cats."

"That's right," he said eagerly. "Did you see my ad or—"

"Actually it was Cara who mentioned it. I was at her Thanksgiving dinner yesterday. We barely met. My name's Beth, and I was there with my daughter, Annabelle. Although Annabelle had her nose in her phone and hardly said a word to anyone."

"Oh yeah," he said. "I know who you are." He remembered the flashy, middle-aged redhead with too much makeup and the teen girl who looked like the poster child for post-Goth.

"Anyway, Cara told me you had cats to give away. And, ever since we moved here, I've been promising Annabelle that she could have a cat."

Garrison cringed to think of the strange-looking girl with multiple piercings taking home one of his cats. But then he chided himself for being too judgmental. After all, he'd gone through some rough teen years himself. "You say you just moved here?" he ventured.

"Oh, it's been a couple years now. I kept making up new excuses not to have a cat. But Annabelle's not letting me off the hook."

He explained a bit about Gram's will. "I know her requirements might sound extravagant to some people, but I have to respect her wishes. Do you mind if I ask a few questions?"

"Not at all." She giggled. "Imagine being interviewed to adopt a cat."

"I know." He pulled out Gram's list and went over the preliminaries, and all seemed to be in order. Beth was a solid candidate. "Sounds good," he told her. "But I'll still need to evaluate your house."

"For what?" she sounded worried.

"To make sure it's a safe, healthy place for a cat."

"Seriously?"

"Yeah, but don't worry. It's not like I'm inspecting your housekeeping."

"Well, like I said, I do hair from my home, so I did pass that inspection."

"That's great," he told her. "Mind if I come by for a quick look? And, trust me, I'm as eager to find homes for these cats as you are to have one of them."

She told him where she lived, and he asked when he should come by.

"Can you do it right now?" she said eagerly. "Annabelle is out and I'd rather she not know about this. I mean, just in case it doesn't work out."

"No problem."

As Garrison hurried the several blocks to Beth's house, he actually shot up a quick prayer for help that this adoption would work out. One less cat would be real progress. And if Beth and Annabelle did qualify, hopefully they wouldn't want Harry. Perhaps Garrison would put Harry out of sight.

Garrison did a quick tour through Beth's house. Although her house was a little messy and cluttered and her breakfast dishes were still in the sink, he felt that the place was just fine for a cat. Before he left, he explained the need for another visitation after a couple of weeks. "I can't tell you exactly what day it will be. It's supposed to be a surprise visitation."

"Are you kidding?" Beth scowled.

"I know it sounds nuts," he admitted. "But can I trust you with a secret?"

Her blue eyes grew wide. "Sure."

"Well, there's a little surprise that comes with the cats. My grandmother wanted to be sure they found good homes."

"And you can't tell me what kind of surprise?" Beth looked curious. "Is it a year's supply of cat food? That would be nice."

"Something like that," he assured her. "But I can't tell you until the cat's been happily homed for at least three weeks."

"I thought you said two weeks?"

He was just finishing his explanation when Annabelle walked in. "What's up?" she asked with a suspicious frown.

"You remember Garrison from Cara's?" Beth said.

Annabelle just nodded.

"He's offered to give you a cat," Beth announced.

Annabelle's face lit up. "Really? I can have a cat?"

"That's right." Beth glanced at Garrison. "I mean, we did fit the criteria, didn't we?"

"What criteria?" Annabelle asked.

"Take it from me," her mom told her. "These must be very special cats. Garrison does not just give them to anyone."

Annabelle seemed to appreciate this. "When do I get it?"

"Is now too soon?" Garrison asked.

"Not at all. Can I get a cat right now?" Annabelle asked her mom.

"Why don't you go home with Garrison? I've got a client coming in a few minutes. Be sure and bring back the pick of the litter."

As they were leaving, Garrison regretted it. This wouldn't give him time to hide Harry. What if Annabelle fell in love with Harry?

Garrison rattled the cat treat bag. Just as expected, the cats began to emerge from their favorite nooks and crannies. Before long he was introducing each feline by name. Annabelle went from cat to cat, carefully examining each of them. However, it was the moody calico that seemed to capture her attention. Annabelle offered Spooky some more cat treats and, to Garrison's surprise, she soon got the temperamental cat to eat right out of her hand.

"I want Spooky," she announced, still holding the cat—who seemed strangely content—in her arms. "Is that okay?"

"That's fine." He grinned. "That's perfect."

"I think she needs me," Annabelle said.

Garrison showed her to the cat pantry, inviting her to pick out some things she might need. He explained about the special drops Spooky needed in her food to prevent hairballs and even gave her a cat bed and a carrying case as well as a bag of kitty litter.

As he drove Annabelle home, Garrison tried to conceal how elated he felt to have the moody feline off his hands. But he was glad for both the girl and the cat—they seemed perfectly simpatico. As he helped Annabelle carry the cat things into her house, she thanked him profusely, acting as if he'd just given her the greatest treasure in the world.

"You're completely welcome," he told her. "Don't forget that I have to come by to check on the cat after two weeks, and then again after three weeks."

"You can come see Spooky whenever you like," she told him. "I can understand how you might miss her. But I promise I'll take really good care of her. Don't worry."

Garrison tried not to laugh as he went back to the car. Annabelle had no idea how relieved he felt. And he knew Gram would be delighted to see how much this young girl loved her new cat.

As Garrison was leaving the church on Sunday, he was approached by an older man. Wearing a worn sports jacket and a tweed driving cap, the man waved to Garrison as if he knew him. "I'm Vincent Peterson," he said eagerly. "We met briefly at Cara's Thanksgiving get-together last week."

"Oh yeah." Garrison nodded, ducking beneath a covered walkway to get out of the rain that was just starting to pelt down. "I thought you looked familiar."

"Cara mentioned that you're looking for homes for your grandmother's cats. I might be interested. That is if you still have any cats left."

"Definitely," Garrison assured him. "I have four."

Vincent looked relieved. "I had a cat named Gracie for years. A big orange cat that I was very attached to. But she got a kidney disease and passed away last winter. I told myself I wouldn't get another cat, but I suppose I'm having second thoughts now."

"Cats can be great companions," Garrison said positively as they moved closer to the wall to escape the windblown rain.

"Yes, I think you're right. And since I'm spending more time at home . . ." He grimly shook his head. "You see, I was forced into retirement last spring. So I find myself rambling around my house. Last week Cara was trying to convince me that I need a cat." He chuckled. "The more I think about it, the more I think she might be right."

Garrison quickly went over the preliminary questions and, convinced that Vincent was a good candidate, he explained about the need for a home visit. Although Vincent looked bewildered by this, he agreed. "Why don't you come over for coffee tomorrow morning," he suggested. "That'll give me a chance to straighten up some."

They agreed on the time and Vincent gave Garrison directions to his house. Garrison tried not to do the Snoopy happy dance as he hurried across the parking lot to the car. If Vincent took a cat, that would leave just three cats to place. And his new ad hadn't even been run in the local paper yet.

As he drove home, he pondered over the fact that Cara had sent two potential cat owners his way. Perhaps she didn't despise him as much as he'd imagined. Or perhaps she was just concerned for the cats in his care. Whatever her motives, he still owed her his gratitude.

On Monday morning, Garrison showed up at Vincent's house at ten o'clock sharp. It was a small, modest, midcentury home, but it was tidy and neat in a plain and simple sort of way.

"Do you mind having coffee in the kitchen?" Vincent asked apologetically. "I'm not used to entertaining much."

"The kitchen is perfect," Garrison told him.

"This isn't exactly how I planned for my life to go," Vincent said as he placed a coffee mug in front of Garrison.

"How so?"

"Well, I had hoped to retire with my wife by my side." He let out a sad sigh as he sat on the other side of the well-worn table. "Lynnette left me about ten years ago. Talk about being blindsided." He took a sip. "Sure didn't see that one coming."

"Sorry about that."

"And then there was my retirement." Another long sigh. "Thought I'd walk away with a nice little package and benefits, you know. Not a windfall, mind you, but enough to do a little traveling or maybe just fix up my little house."

"That didn't happen?"

Vincent let out a sarcastic laugh. "Not hardly. Seems the

economy is responsible for my loss. Anyway that's what I was told. Didn't even get a gold watch. But I guess that's not so unusual these days."

"That's too bad."

He shrugged. "I suppose I should consider myself lucky to still have this house." He glanced around. "I know it's not much, but at least it's mine. Just wish I could afford to do some improvements though. I'm pretty handy with hammer and nails."

"Well, the house looks sturdy enough," Garrison observed. Then he explained about how he was doing some much-needed repairs to Gram's house. "But I have to admit I don't really know what I'm doing."

Vincent's brows arched. "Well, if you need any help, just call."

"Really?" Garrison studied him, gauging if this offer was just casual friendliness or something he could depend upon.

He nodded. "You bet. At the very least I can give you some pointers and tips. And I've got lots of time."

"That'd be great, Vincent. I'll take you up on it." Garrison described some of the projects he wanted to complete before it was time to return to Seattle, and Vincent had some brilliant suggestions. He even pulled out some do-it-yourself books for Garrison to take with him. Then they arranged for Vincent to come over and see the cats in the afternoon.

"And maybe you can show me how to fix that door that sticks," Garrison said hopefully.

"You got it."

As Garrison drove home, he wondered if it would be selfish to hide Harry in the laundry room when Vincent came to view the cats. Yet, at the same time, he knew that was silly.

Besides that, Vincent seemed like a nice guy. He would probably provide a great home for a nice cat like Harry.

Vincent showed up around one, just as Garrison was finishing up painting a wall in the kitchen. He'd chosen a nice buttery yellow that really warmed the room up. It was the first time he'd ever painted anything, and he didn't want to admit it, but he felt pretty pleased with himself.

"That looks good," Vincent told him as Garrison showed him his work. "But it would be a lot quicker and easier if you used masking tape."

"Masking tape?" Garrison frowned.

Vincent explained how to tape off areas that weren't in need of paint. "Like that baseboard there."

Garrison laughed as he pulled out a brand-new roll of blue tape. "So that's why the guy at the paint store insisted I buy this. I could blame my ignorance on Uganda. I spent the last nine years there and sometimes I feel like I'm still catching up on American culture."

Vincent showed how to mask off the cabinets and a couple of other tricks.

"I'm going to have to put you on speed dial," Garrison said as he set his paintbrush aside. "Now would you like to meet the cats?"

"Absolutely."

Garrison led him into the living room where the cats usually hung out. Harry was the first one to approach them, rubbing himself affectionately against Garrison's legs. "This is Harry. He's a Maine Coon cat and, in my opinion, the pick of the litter." He chuckled as he bent down to scratch the top of Harry's head.

"Handsome fellow." Vincent nodded with approval.

"And this is Muzzy." Garrison pointed to the oversized Siamese who immediately began "talking" in loud meows. "She's very social. As you can see, she likes to talk."

"She's a pretty cat," Vincent said. "But I'm not overly fond of the Siamese breed." He went over to the chair where Rusty and Oreo were snuggled up together. "And these cats?"

"They're both males," Garrison said. "The black-and-white is Oreo. This one lives to eat and could probably get a lifetime membership in Overeaters Anonymous. He always thinks it's dinnertime. The orange one is Rusty. They both have wonderful dispositions. Good-natured and easygoing and friendly."

"Rusty?" Vincent picked up the big orange cat. "You're a big guy, Rusty," he said in a friendly tone.

Garrison could hear the cat purring happily. "Rusty is ten years old. No health problems. My grandmother took him in about six years ago."

"You want to go home with me, big boy? Leave your cat friends behind?"

"All his friends are relocating," Garrison reminded him. "That is, unless you'd like more than just one cat?"

"Oh no, I don't think so."

Garrison was highly tempted to tell Vincent about the cash prize that was attached to each cat. He suspected Vincent could really use the money. But at the same time, it seemed unfair to tip his hand like this. Perhaps it was better for people to make up their minds about the cats without any extra incentive. That was probably the way Gram had wanted it.

Vincent grinned down at Rusty. "I thought I wanted a female cat, but maybe I was wrong. You seem like a good pal to me."

Rusty looked perfectly content. In fact, unless it was Garrison's imagination, he almost seemed to be smiling. "Well, I think you've made a friend," Garrison said to both of them. He explained about the two- and four-week visitations. "I know it sounds a little goofy," he said quickly. "But my grandmother was really attached to her cats. They were like her children. She just wanted to ensure their future."

"I don't mind a bit," Vincent told him. "It's been a little lonely at my house. I'd welcome your visits. And, like I said, I'm available to help with your home improvements. Just give me a call."

Garrison led Vincent to the cat pantry. "Feel free to take some things for Rusty." He explained Rusty's dietary preferences, removing an eight-pack of cat food cans as well as some other things. "And there's a cat carrier out on the porch."

Before long, Vincent and Rusty were happily headed out the door. Garrison watched as Vincent drove the car away. "Three down, three to go," he said as he closed the door. "Not bad for just over a week."

As he returned to painting, he knew he really owed Cara one. Make that two, since both Spooky and Rusty had found homes thanks to her intervention. He wondered how he could express his gratitude to her without offending her. He also wondered if there was any way to win her friendship . . . short of handing over Harry. As willing as he was to do just that—really there was no one else he'd rather give Harry to—he knew he had to honor Gram's wishes.

Garrison finished up the walls in the kitchen. After giving the cats each a kitty treat and promising to be back soon, he cleaned himself up and drove Gram's old car to town. His goal was to get a nice bouquet of flowers for Cara. His way to thank her—both for Thanksgiving dinner and for her help finding homes for Rusty and Spooky.

At the florist, he looked long and hard at the arrangements. He didn't want to get anything too romantic—like roses—because he felt certain that would scare her off even more. He just wanted something pleasant and unassuming. Finally he decided on a sizeable pink poinsettia plant that was prettily potted in a large metallic green container. Very festive and Christmassy. It would look nice on her big, round dining table. He also found a card that he took the time to write inside. Nothing too familiar or presuming—but just casually friendly and grateful.

"I'm going to make it a hood," the saleswoman told him as he was pocketing his receipt.

"A hood?"

She pulled out a long strip of brown paper. "To protect it from the chilly air as you transport it to the car."

"Huh?" Sometimes he felt like an alien from a different planet. Since when did plants start wearing clothing?

"Poinsettias are very sensitive to the cold. Make sure you get it directly into the house. Otherwise the petals will fall off."

He blinked. "The petals will fall off?"

She nodded grimly. "Yes. And we have a no-return policy."

"Right . . ."

"Is it a gift?" she asked as she taped the "hood" loosely around the plant.

"Yes, as a matter of fact."

"Well, whatever you do, don't leave it by the front door. That would kill it for sure."

"Right." He hadn't realized a poinsettia was so temperamental.

"Does the person you're giving it to have pets or small children?"

"No."

"Good. Poinsettia leaves are poisonous if ingested."

"Yeah, well, I doubt she will eat it."

The woman laughed.

Garrison was tempted to tell the woman he had changed his mind. Who knew a simple plant could be such high maintenance? Almost as bad as a houseful of cats.

"Well, I hope she enjoys it. It's really a lovely gift."

Garrison carefully picked up the plant. "Thanks. I hope I can get it safely to her."

She waved her hand. “Don’t worry. I probably made it sound worse than it is. Just be careful with the cold air.”

He hurried the delicate plant out to his car and, fastening the seatbelt around it, he quickly started the car and cranked up the heat. As he drove to Cara’s house, he wondered what he’d do if she wasn’t home. At first he had hoped she would be gone so that he could leave it on her porch. Now he wasn’t so sure. Perhaps he could leave it with a neighbor? Or else he could take it home with him. Except that it might poison the cats.

Feeling a bit silly and uneasy, Garrison pulled into her driveway and carefully extracted the plant from the car, hurrying to take it up to the front porch where he rang the doorbell. When no one answered, he looked down at the bundle in his arms. He longed to just leave it, but the image of Cara discovering a dead plant on her porch was definitely not a good one.

“Hello?” a male voice called from the house next door. “Are you looking for Cara?”

“Yes,” Garrison said eagerly. “I have something for her, but she doesn’t seem to be at home and I don’t want to leave it on the porch.”

“You can leave it with me if you like.” The guy waved him over. “Cara and I are good friends. She’s usually home, but Monday is her day to go into the office. If you like, I can take it over to her when she gets home.”

“Great!” Garrison hurried over to the tan house next door. “I’d leave it on her porch, but the flowers can’t handle the cold.”

“Are you a delivery man from the florist?” The neighbor glanced over at the old Pontiac with interest. “That doesn’t look like their usual van.”

"No, I'm just a friend of Cara's." Okay, Garrison knew that was a stretch. "A relatively new acquaintance actually."

"I'm David Landers." He smiled as he extended his hand.

"I'm Garrison Brown. I live a few blocks from here."

"Nice to meet you, neighbor." David appeared to be about the same age as Garrison, but unlike Garrison, this guy oozed confidence.

"Yeah. Thanks." Garrison held out the plant. "And thanks for taking—"

"Why don't you come on in?" David opened the door wider.

"Okay." Garrison was pleasantly surprised at this unexpected hospitality. "I didn't realize poinsettias were so fragile when I bought this."

"No problem." David closed the door and pointed to a glass-topped table in the foyer. "Just set it there for now. I'll get it to Cara as soon as she gets home. Probably around five." He grinned. "I like having an excuse to run over and see her whenever I can. When she first moved in, she used to come over here a lot to borrow stuff. It's her first time living in a real house and she'd need a potato peeler or some basil or whatever. I didn't mind a bit. After she got settled, I missed her visits so I started making up reasons to pop in on her." He chuckled. "But we're beyond that now."

"Right . . ." For some reason Garrison felt uncomfortable hearing this.

"How do you know Cara?" David gave him an overly curious look.

Garrison gauged his answer. "We met on the street just last week. And then my neighbor took me over to Cara's for Thanksgiving—a get-together for the single folks in the neighborhood." He studied David closely, trying to calculate his age. Somewhere between thirty-five and forty, he would estimate. "I don't believe you were there." He glanced around the homey-looking room. "But maybe you're not single."

"I'm divorced. Three years last summer. And I would've gone to Cara's little shindig, but I had a previous commitment with my family in Spokane. My parents wanted to see Jackson."

"Jackson?"

"That's my son. I have full custody of the kid. Jackson just turned eight." He called over his shoulder. "Hey, Jackson? You still in the kitchen? Come on out here."

A young boy came shyly around a corner, peering into the living room.

"Say hello to Mr. Brown." David looked uncertainly at Garrison. "It was Brown, wasn't it?"

"Yes." Garrison smiled at the boy. "Hello, Jackson."

"He-hello," the boy said with uncertainty.

"Mr. Brown brought a plant over for Miss Wilson," David told his son.

Jackson just nodded as he moved toward the staircase, nervously grasping the banister with one hand. "I—uh—I'm going—to my room."

"Okay," David said easily.

"Nice to meet you, Jackson," Garrison called out as the boy scurried up the stairs.

David frowned. "I like to give him every opportunity I can to interact."

"Sure." Garrison pretended to understand, although he wasn't completely sure what David meant.

"Because, as you can probably see, Jackson has difficulty

conversing," David continued quietly. "They say he's got a social anxiety disorder. But things got worse when kids at school started teasing him. So I took him out. I don't mind homeschooling so much since I work from home anyway. And Jackson is really bright. But I do worry about his social interaction. I wish he had someone his own age to talk with."

Garrison nodded, realizing that he could probably relate more to David's insecure son than to the self-assured dad. "Yeah, that would probably be good for him."

"I'm thinking about getting him a dog for Christmas. Although I need to make sure our budget can handle it. It hasn't been exactly easy getting my home business up and running. And I know dogs can be expensive. But it might be worth it . . . for Jackson's sake. Not that a dog can carry on a conversation exactly." David pulled back a corner of the brown paper hood to peek in on the poinsettia. "Pretty."

"How about a cat?" Garrison said suddenly.

"Huh?" David's brow creased as he pushed the paper closed again. "A cat?"

Garrison quickly explained about Gram and her cats and the need to re-home them. "I still have this Seal Point Siamese. About eight years old. Nice and big. And she talks *all the time*."

"She *talks*?" David looked skeptical.

"I know it sounds crazy, but this cat *talks*. In cat language, of course, but she's really chatty. I have a feeling she carried on lengthy conversations with my grandmother." He shrugged. "Unfortunately, I'm not great at conversing with cats. I'm sure poor Muzzy is completely fed up with me."

"A Seal Point Siamese? I've seen pictures of those. Nice-looking cats."

"Muzzy is really pretty. Nice, sleek dark coat. Big blue eyes. And like I said, she loves to talk."

"Eight years? Is that very old? I mean, for a cat?"

"My grandmother had a cat named Genevieve that lived to be twenty-three."

"No kidding." David shook his head. "And Jackson is eight years old—just like Muzzy."

"No worries that she'll have kittens," Garrison assured him. "And she's in good health. I have the vet records."

David narrowed his eyes as if really considering this. "You really think this cat could encourage Jackson to talk more?"

"I'm almost certain of it. The cat really wants to engage with someone. She's a real chatterbox." He didn't add that she could drive a quiet person crazy. Let them discover this. Besides, it was clear that David liked to chat.

"And a cat wouldn't pass judgment on Jackson."

"Not at all. And she'd be a good companion for him too."

"I like this idea." David nodded. "I like it a lot."

Garrison told David a bit about his grandmother's will. "I know it sounds a little eccentric, but Gram's cats were her family. She had to make sure they got good homes."

"I don't blame her a bit." David invited Garrison to remove his coat and sit down to go over the details of Gram's slightly eccentric requirements.

It didn't take long for Garrison to realize that this would be a great home for Muzzy. "And I know my grandmother would be pleased to think that Muzzy could be an encouragement to your boy."

"I want to do this," David declared. "It makes perfect sense. Jackson isn't getting a dog for Christmas. He's getting a cat."

"Great." Garrison frowned. "But I hope you don't want to wait until Christmas."

"Why not?"

"Well, I'm trying to get things tied up before that. I actually hoped to get the cats placed this week. And then I have to head back to Seattle for a job. I'd been looking for months and finally got an offer. Can't afford to let it go."

"Sure." David nodded. "I can understand that. And, come to think of it, I've heard that you should never give pets right at Christmas. Too much going on. They can get stressed out . . . or sick."

"So would you be interested in getting Muzzy sooner then?"

"Sure. Why not?"

"I could bring her by anytime you want," Garrison offered. "Well, unless you'd like to meet her first. Or maybe you want to talk to Jackson—"

"No, I think I'd rather surprise him."

"I can show you a picture." Garrison pulled his phone from his pocket. "I've got photos of all the cats on here."

David peered over Garrison's shoulder as he flicked through the photos. "There's Muzzy." Garrison held up the phone.

"She is a pretty cat." David smiled with satisfaction. "And you mentioned the two-week policy . . . Can I assume it works both ways?"

"Both ways?"

"If Muzzy doesn't fit in here. If she and Jackson don't hit it off—I can send her back?"

Garrison considered this. "Sure, of course. I know that my grandmother would not want Muzzy placed in a home that didn't work for everyone."

David stuck out his hand. "Then it's a deal."

"Deal." Garrison grinned.

"When can we have her?"

"If you like I can bring her over tonight."

"That'd be great."

Garrison felt like letting out a victory yell as he hurried out to his car. Finding a home for Muzzy—a cat whose constant "talking" was driving him up the walls—was fantastic. And if she could help Jackson with his social anxiety—well, it was a real win-win situation. At home, he felt slightly guilty as he gathered up a generous supply of cat things for Muzzy. It wasn't that he disliked the loud Siamese so much. In fact, she'd actually grown on him the last few days. But at the same time, he knew she needed a good home. Just the right kind of home. And he felt fairly certain he had found it.

Using a special gluten-free kitty treat to entice Muzzy into a cat carrier, he assured her that she was going to a happy home with a young man who would adore her. With her safely away from the other cats, he took a moment to give the others their dinner. Then he packed a box with everything a new cat owner could possibly want, including a nearly full bag of her special cat food, and loaded it into the back of the Pontiac. With the cat carrier safely buckled into the seat next to him, he drove over to David's. Was it really possible he was down to just two cats? Not to mention they were two of the most congenial cats. Finding them homes should be a piece of cake.

Feeling hopeful and optimistic, Garrison toted the cat carrier up to the front door of the Landerses' house. From the corner of his eye, he noticed a car pulling into Cara's driveway. Glancing over, he watched as the sky-blue Volkswagen Bug parked. While knocking on the door, he watched Cara climb out of her car and look curiously in his direction. Smiling, he waved, then knocked on the door again. It opened a moment later.

"Is this her? Is this Muzzy?" David asked expectantly.

"Is that the cat?" Jackson asked from behind his dad.

"This is Muzzy," Garrison proclaimed.

"Here's your early Christmas present, Jackson." David took the carrier from Garrison and held it out in front of his son. "Your very own cat. Meet Muzzy."

"I'm going back to the car for some things," Garrison called out to them. As he turned away he could hear the happiness in Jackson's voice. The boy was clearly thrilled to be getting a cat. It was like Christmas had come early.

"What's going on over there?" Cara asked with a curious expression.

Garrison quickly explained about finding a home for a cat.

Her brows arched. "Really? Which cat?"

"Muzzy," he said as he reached in for the box of cat supplies. "The Siamese."

Cara smiled stiffly. "Well, that's very nice." She took a shopping bag out of her car. "Nice to see you, Garrison." Then she turned and hurried up to her house. Friendly . . . but cool.

Garrison returned to the Landerses' house, depositing the box inside the door and going over some particulars about their new cat, including her need for a gluten-free diet. At least they wouldn't have to worry about her sneaking food from the other cats and getting sick. Muzzy was on her own here. And already she was comfortably seated in Jackson's lap, and he was happily stroking her sleek dark coat.

"I'll leave you to it." Garrison reached for the poinsettia plant, still on the foyer table.

"You're taking that back?" David looked concerned.

"Cara's home now," Garrison told him. "I'll just take it over."

"Oh . . . okay." David frowned. "But I'm happy to—"

"No problem," Garrison said lightly. "I already said hello to her. I'll just run it over while I'm here."

David just nodded, but he didn't seem overly pleased. He had probably been looking forward to another excuse to pop in on his neighbor. Maybe their relationship wasn't as solid as David had made it seem. Or maybe it was. Maybe he felt jealous of Garrison's interest in her now. Wouldn't that be a twist.

"Thanks so much for the cat." David shook his hand. "I really appreciate it."

"Yeah," Jackson said with glowing eyes. "Thanks, Mister, uh, Brown. Thanks a lot."

"You're more than welcome, Jackson. I think my grandmother would be really pleased to see that Muzzy has found such a good home. I hope you really enjoy each other."

As Garrison carried his paper-covered poinsettia plant over to Cara's he had a sense of real accomplishment. But at the same time he felt uneasy. Maybe it was a mistake trying to befriend Cara like this. She seemed to be making herself clear—she had no interest in being anything more than a cool and casual acquaintance with him. Maybe he should just take a hint.

"For me?" Cara looked truly surprised as he handed her the hooded planter and card.

"Yes." He forced a nervous smile. "To show my gratitude."

"Gratitude for what?"

"For sharing Thanksgiving dinner with me," he said sheepishly, "although I suspect you hadn't really meant to have me in your home. More than that, it's to say thanks for encouraging your friends—Beth and Annabelle and Vincent—to adopt cats from me."

She shrugged. "Oh . . . well . . ."

"I really appreciate you connecting them to me."

"They just seemed like good candidates." She made a smirk at him. "Unlike me."

Garrison felt deflated.

"Sorry," she said quickly. "I didn't mean to go there." She

gave him a genuine smile. "Why don't you come inside? It's cold out here. And I'd like to see what's in this package."

He felt instantly at home inside her house. And he was amused to see that it was actually bigger than it had seemed on Thanksgiving. "You have a really nice place," he said as she set the package on a coffee table and opened the card.

"Thanks." She nodded, then held up the card. "And thanks for this too." She leaned over and peeled the hood from the plant. To Garrison's relief the delicate pink blossoms were all still intact. "Why, it's beautiful," she gushed. "But you really didn't have to—"

"I wanted to," he clarified. "I felt like we got off on the wrong foot. And, well, since we're neighbors and all. And you've been such an asset in finding homes for my cats. Even discovering your neighbor David today came as a result of trying to drop this plant by your house."

"And he really took a cat?" she said with interest.

Garrison explained about Muzzy's chattiness and how she seemed a good match for Jackson. "I thought Muzzy might get him to relax and talk more . . . you know?"

"That's brilliant!" She picked up the poinsettia plant, carried it to her dining area, and, just like Garrison had imagined, she placed it on the dark-stained table. "Perfect."

"I couldn't agree more." He smiled. "Now I should let you get back to whatever you were doing."

"Just putting away groceries," she said as she went into the kitchen. "There's this great natural food store down the street from my employer. And since I have to go into the office on Mondays, I usually stock up."

"David mentioned that you had meetings on Mondays." He didn't know what to do, so he followed her into the kitchen.

It was small and old-fashioned, similar to Gram's. Except that it was in better shape.

"Dear David," she said as she removed an acorn squash from her cloth shopping bag. "I'm so lucky to have him next door."

"He seems to feel the same," Garrison admitted.

She studied him as she took out a large red onion. "Yes, it's nice to have good neighbors . . . don't you think?"

"Absolutely. I adore Ruby."

"She is a dear."

"And it seems obvious that you've made lots of friends in the neighborhood." He watched as she set some really nice-looking tomatoes on the tile-topped counter.

"You mean for a newcomer?" she teased.

"Yes . . . well, you know what I mean."

"Uh-huh. I'd venture to say I know more people in this neighborhood than you do."

"I'm sure that's true. Although, at the rate I'm going—finding homes for these cats—I might catch up."

"Well, except that you must be nearly out of cats. How many do you have left?"

"Just two. Oreo and Harry."

"Right . . ."

"And in my opinion they are the best ones of the batch. They should be easy to place."

"No doubt." She set a pair of zucchinis on the counter and smiled. "Well, thanks so much for the lovely poinsettia. It really brightens up the place. Puts me in the Christmas spirit." She narrowed her eyes slightly. "Now if I could just find myself a good cat."

Garrison cringed. "Okay, I get the hint."

"Sorry . . ." She held up her hands. "I know I can be a terrible tease sometimes." She walked up close to him and looked directly into his eyes. "Really, no hard feelings. Okay?"

He tilted his head to one side as if unconvinced. "I don't know . . ."

"What?"

"I'm not so sure I can trust you, Cara. You seem intent on harboring resentments against me. I'm beginning to think you'll never forgive me."

"Of course, I forgive you, Garrison. I'm just giving you a hard time."

"I don't know about that," he said in a slightly taunting tone. "A guy could take it personally."

"Well, that's ridiculous. I was just jerking your chain. I'm completely over the whole business with the cat and—"

"I might need more convincing," he said.

"Huh?"

"If you've really forgiven me, Cara, how about if you . . . say . . . went out to dinner with me?" He cringed inwardly. Had he really just said that?

"What?" She frowned. "Is this some kind of dating blackmail?"

He grinned nervously. "Maybe. Although I've never resorted to blackmail dates before." The truth was that his dating experience was embarrassingly limited.

She looked at the produce spread over her counter. "When do you want to go for dinner?" she asked.

"You name it."

She gave him a doubtful look. "Tonight?"

He concealed his surprise. "Sure, tonight is great. No problem."

"Good." She folded the bag and nodded firmly. "Despite collecting all these yummy vegetables today, I really didn't feel like cooking. It's been a long day."

As they put on their coats, Garrison could not believe his luck. Cara had actually agreed to go to dinner with him. Okay, maybe she just didn't want to cook at home, but what difference did it make? This was his chance to get to know her better. And maybe this meant that she and her neighbor David weren't as involved as he had assumed they were. Maybe he really did have a chance. Now if he could just not blow it.

"Do you mind if we meet there?" she asked as they went outside.

He tried not to look disappointed. "Are you afraid of my grandmother's old Pontiac?" He tipped his head to David's driveway where his car was still parked. Suddenly he was more aware than ever of the dull green paint, the dent in the right fender. He knew a little paint and TLC could turn the car into a real gem, but right now she looked pretty forlorn—although the interior was in good shape.

"No. I just like feeling independent." Cara tilted her chin up. "I'll have my own wheels—just in case we both decide we can't stand each other after all."

He frowned. "You really think that's going to happen?"

"You never can tell." She gave him a cheesy grin as she opened her car door. "I mean, if I'm not good enough for your cat, how could I be good enough for you?"

"But you said you'd—"

"Meet you at Fowlers'," she called as she closed her door.

He nodded. Fowlers' Fish House? That's where she wanted to go on their "first date"? Okay, he reminded himself, maybe this wasn't really a date. Maybe it was more like two people getting better acquainted over fish and chips. An icy rain was coming down as he drove to town. A night not fit for man or beasts. But he was not going to back down due to bad weather. And by the time he parked in front of Fowlers', which did not look very busy, a steaming bowl of chowder was starting to sound pretty good.

He jogged through the rain and caught up with her as she was going in the door. The whole restaurant was glowing, both inside and outside, with hundreds of multi-colored Christmas lights. The sight of a gaudily decorated fake tree and the smell of fried fish greeted him as he went inside. Everywhere he looked were the bright trappings and trimmings of Christmas. As a child he would've loved this. As an adult, it was a little over the top. But at least it was warm in here. That was something.

"Festive," he told Cara as he peeled off his coat.

She pointed to a glossy pine picnic table next to the window. "That okay?"

"Sure." He followed her over to the table and sat down across from her. "I haven't been here in years," he confessed. "But I used to like this place when I was a kid."

"I consider Fowlers' as one of my guilty pleasures," she said as she unwound a bright red scarf from around her neck.

"Why a guilty pleasure?"

"I heard how many calories are in their fish basket." As she reached for a greasy menu, she wrinkled her nose. Totally endearing. "As a result, I try to limit myself to only once a week."

"Right." He nodded. "Although I'm not sure why you're

concerned about calories. Frankly, after seeing all that produce in your kitchen, I'm relieved you're not a vegetarian or vegan or something like that."

She laughed. "No, I tried being a vegan briefly after college, but my hair started to fall out. However, I do try to eat my vegetables." Her smile faded. "That's something my mom always tried to get me to do . . . when she was alive. I didn't do such a great job then, but I'm trying to make up for it now."

"I'm sorry." He peered at her. "Has she been gone for long?"

"I was in my second year at college when she was diagnosed." She pulled a napkin out of the container, using it to wipe wet raindrops from her face. "Just the age when I was really starting to appreciate my mom. She battled cancer for about three years. She made it to my graduation . . . but not long after that."

"That's hard," he said sadly. "I kind of know how you feel. I lost both of my parents when I was twelve."

"Really?" Her eyes widened. "I'm sorry. I had no idea."

"Yeah . . . my grandma took me in. I was quite a handful. But my grandma—she was a really special lady. I honestly don't know where I'd be without her."

Her brown eyes grew warmer and softer. "And that's why you want to honor her wishes with her cats."

He nodded soberly. "Even when it's not easy."

"Well, that's very respectable, Garrison. I'm sorry I was such a pill about Harry. I hope you find him the perfect home."

Garrison talked a little about the recent cat placements and how they all seemed to be working out perfectly. "Almost like

Gram is up there in heaven orchestrating the whole thing." He smiled at Cara. "Or like she sent me an angel to help out. Again, I have to thank you."

"I'm happy to be of help. And that reminds me. I have another friend and I think she might be perfect for a cat. In fact, she would probably fall in love with Harry."

He nodded, but felt a small wave of uncertainty. As badly as he wanted to be rid of the cats and to sell Gram's house and to be on his way, he knew he was getting attached to that big Maine Coon cat. "Who is that?" he asked carefully.

"Her name is Sabrina," Cara began. "She's a real sweetheart."

"And she lives in our neighborhood."

"Yes. That's how we met. She lives on the street behind me. We share the same backyard fence. Her yard is absolutely gorgeous and she's promised to give me gardening tips next spring."

"Sounds like a nice neighbor."

"Yes. Sabrina is one of those women who can do everything. I mean, she cooks and gardens and sews and does crafts—the works. She's been a real inspiration to me."

"Sounds like she's a busy woman. Does she have a job?"

"She works from her home. As a seamstress. She does alterations and things like that. Her husband, Riley, manages an appliance store. They are like this sweet, old-fashioned couple, but they're our age."

"Our age?"

"You know . . . thirty-something." She grinned. "Riley might be pushing forty. But Sabrina has to be midthirties."

"Yeah." He nodded. "And do they have a solid marriage? Or do you know?"

"Very solid. Their biggest problem is that they can't have kids. Sounds like they've spent lots of money trying to. Sabrina is trying to resign herself to it, but I know it's been hard on her. I've been telling her she should get some pets. But she doesn't like dogs."

"Does she like cats?"

Cara shrugged. "I'm not sure. All I know is that she does not like dogs. One of our neighbors has several and she sometimes complains about what they do to her yard."

They chatted on and on as they ate fish and chips and chowder. And by the time they were done, Garrison felt like he'd made real progress.

"Friends?" he said as they prepared to leave the restaurant.

"Friends," she declared as she held out her hand. He grasped it and shook it.

"That's a relief. I was afraid you were never going to get over losing Harry," he confessed.

Her dark eyes twinkled. "Well, I now have a plan for Harry's future. I'm hoping he'll become my neighbor and I'll get to spend lots of time with him."

"You talk to Sabrina and we'll see how it goes," he said as they stepped out into the cold.

"Thanks for dinner," she called out as she pulled her scarf over her head and got ready to dash through the rain.

"Thank *you*!" Garrison took off after her, waving as they parted ways at their cars. That had gone well. Really, really well. As he started the Pontiac's engine, he looked at the funky old fish house and grinned. What a perfect place for a first date! Cara had been a genius to choose it. Why had he been so doubtful? And Fowlers' looked really beautiful from the car. Against the blackness of a dark rainy night, dozens of strings of colorful lights were cheerfully reflected in the shining puddles, doubling the effects of the rainbows of light. Even the inflated vinyl Santa standing next to the giant anchor had a certain charm. For some reason everything looked better to him now.

The next morning, Garrison was surprised to hear someone knocking at the back door. It was barely seven. He hurried past where Oreo and Harry were already waiting for breakfast and pulled open the door. "Ruby?" he peered curiously at his bathrobe-clad neighbor. "What are you doing out this early?"

She held out what looked like a covered plate. "Breakfast," she told him with a wide grin.

"Seriously?" He moved back, welcoming her into the house. "What did I do to deserve this?"

"Just being neighborly," she said as she set the oversized plate on the kitchen table, proudly removing the cover. "Ham and eggs. Biscuits and gravy. And grits."

His eyes opened wide and his mouth started to water. *"Grits?"*

She nodded knowingly.

"I haven't had grits in years." He smiled at her. "Not since I lived here and used to sneak over to eat them from your table."

"That's what I figured." She pulled out a chair. "Go ahead, eat it while it's hot."

"Don't mind if I do." He sat down and she handed him silverware from the drawer.

"Dig in and enjoy, Garrison."

"What about your breakfast?" he asked as he stuck his spoon into the grits.

"I already ate. Don't mind me. I'll just make us some coffee."

"Why are you being so nice to me, Ruby?"

"Just being neighborly," she said again. "Neighbors helping neighbors. That's what we do around here."

"Uh-huh." He nodded as he chewed a bite of ham, watching her with suspicion. She was up to something and he knew it. But whatever it was, he didn't think he cared. He hadn't had a breakfast this good in—years!

He was just finishing up the grits when she set a mug of steaming coffee in front of him. She had a cup of her own and sat down with a humph across from him. "Well, how do you like it? Can Ruby still cook grits or not?"

"Oh yeah," he murmured contentedly. "No doubt about it. Ruby still can."

She chuckled, then sipped her coffee.

He was almost done with the biscuits and gravy when she cleared her throat. "Elliott came by last night."

"Your house?"

"Yeah. He spent the night. Still sleeping."

"Uh-huh?"

"I could hardly sleep myself last night. Fretting and worrying over that boy. He's broke with no place to go. Down and out. I just don't know what's to become of him." She sighed. "His clothes were filthy. I've already run them through the washer twice. Once last night. And again this morning. Don't know if they'll ever come clean."

"Clothes can be replaced." He pushed the empty plate aside and reached for his coffee.

"I *know* that." She gave him an exasperated look. "But grandsons cannot."

"Yeah." He nodded. "That's true."

"So I got myself to thinking . . . in the middle of the night . . . after I spent more'n an hour praying to the good Lord to do something about this. I got to thinking that maybe there's something we can do right here. Right under our noses."

"What would that be?"

"Well, I know you're working real hard to fix up Lilly's house. And I got to thinking maybe you could use a spare set of hands." She leaned forward. "Elliott's a strong boy. He can work hard when he sets his mind on it. I thought if he could come over here and help out, well, maybe it would do both you and him some good. What d'you think?"

He chuckled. "I think this breakfast was a bribe."

"Not a bribe exactly. But I thought it might get your undivided attention." She pointed to the empty plate. "Looks like it did too."

"And I'm not complaining either." He smiled at her. "But you didn't need to bring me breakfast, Ruby. I'm happy to hire Elliott. I really could use some help. But I can't afford to pay him much right now."

"I don't want you to pay him at all."

"Why not?"

"Don't want that boy having any money in his pocket. The longer he's broke, the longer he'll stay put."

"I see."

"When it's time to pay him . . . I'll let you know."

"What will I tell him?"

"Don't you worry about that. I'll handle everything." She finished the last of her coffee. "I'll tell him that I'm his manager. If a boy can't trust his grandmother, who can he trust?"

"Good point."

"So . . . if I can get him up—and that might be like raising the dead—I'll get some food into him and send him over here."

"Great." He stood up and rinsed the plate, then handed it back to her. "And thanks for breakfast. I can't remember when I've had a better one."

She reached up and patted his cheek. "You're a sweet boy, Garrison. I sure have missed you."

A couple hours passed before Elliott showed up at the back door—wearing low-slung pants, a ripped T-shirt, a knitted black ski cap, and a suspicious dark scowl. He looked around the kitchen with narrowed eyes. "Just what am I supposed to do anyway?"

Garrison reintroduced himself to the sulky boy, then explained his basic plans for fixing up the house. "I've made a long list." He nodded to the fridge.

"This is all about cats."

"The *other* list. Anyway, right now I need you to help me in getting the living room ready to paint. I want to take the drapes down and mask off the woodwork. After that, you can attack the bathroom." Garrison pulled a fresh particle mask out of a drawer and slipped it on.

"What's that?" Elliott frowned. "We working with toxic stuff or something?"

"No. I just have cat allergies. I take meds, but the masks help too." He jangled another one. "You can wear one if you want, but they get pretty stuffy."

Elliott shook his head then rambled into the living room where the two of them started to remove the dusty drapes and drapery rods. Next Garrison showed Elliott how to mask off the wood, explaining how it was important to get it straight and seal it tight and smooth. Elliott acted nonchalant, but when he started doing it, he took the time to do it right. Garrison could tell this kid was smart. Okay, maybe he wasn't smart when it came to life choices, but he had brains.

"Nice work," he told Elliott when they finished prepping the living room.

Elliott just shrugged. "No big deal."

"Actually, it's a big deal to me," Garrison corrected. "A lot of guys wouldn't do it half as well. I can tell you're intelligent."

Elliott's eyes seemed to light up and then he frowned again. "You mean for a black kid?"

Garrison laughed. "No, that's not what I meant at all. Just take a compliment for what it's worth, okay?"

He shrugged again. "Okay."

"Now if you could go tape off the bathroom beneath the staircase"—he pointed to the door—"just like you did in here, I'd appreciate it."

As Elliott meandered toward the bathroom, Garrison noticed a strange car in front of the house. A pair of women emerged and he felt a surge of happiness to realize that one of them was Cara. The other was a petite blonde woman. "Come in," he called as he opened the front door.

Cara quickly introduced him to Sabrina. "As it turns out, she is interested in getting a cat," she told him. "I hope you don't mind that we popped in."

"Not at all. I'd offer you a chair, but you can see there's a shortage."

"We just came to see the cats," Sabrina said.

"Harry in particular," Cara added.

Garrison went for the bag of cat treats, rattling the plastic and calling until both Harry and Oreo magically appeared. Harry, as usual, rubbed against his legs, looking up with adoring green eyes. Garrison bent down to scratch his head and chin. "Just two boys left," he told Sabrina, "but if you ask me they're the best of the lot."

"Harry is a Maine Coon cat," Cara said with enthusiasm. She knelt down next to Garrison, stroking Harry's silky coat. "They are the best cats ever. Very smart and loyal and, in my opinion, gorgeous."

"He is pretty," Sabrina agreed as she petted the other cat. "But so are you, Oreo."

"Handsome Harry," Cara cooed. Then standing, she glanced around the room. "Are you painting?"

"Yeah." Garrison picked up the paint samples, fanning the colors out. "Now if I could just pick a color."

Cara grimaced. "I wouldn't know where to begin." She pointed to Sabrina, who had squatted down to examine the cats. "She's the real color expert. You should get her opinion." She glanced at her watch. "Now if you guys will excuse me, I have to get home for a conference call at ten. I'll just walk back."

"Thanks for coming with me." Sabrina stood and looked at the color cards in Garrison's hands. "You really want help with that?"

"I would be truly grateful." He handed them over to her and she began walking around the room, taking it all in.

"Is this carpet staying?"

"No way," he assured her. "I'm just leaving it in until I finish painting. Thought it might protect the floors. They're hardwood underneath. I took a peek yesterday and they appear to be in good shape. This house belonged to my grandfather's parents originally and finally to just my grandmother. But I think the carpet was installed back in the sixties." He went over to peel back the corner for her to see.

"Pretty," she said. "It's a lighter wood than I'd have expected. But it'll brighten it up in here. I really like this color." Sabrina pointed to a warm shade of gray. "It's neutral but sophisticated, and it looks really handsome against the dark woodwork. See?" She held it against the wall then handed it back to him.

Garrison studied the color. "I never would've picked that color, but I do like it." He left the card sticking out. "Want to help me with the other rooms?" he asked hopefully.

"Sure. It's the least I can do in exchange for a cat."

"Great. Did you decide on which one?"

She pointed to Oreo. "This guy had me from the get-go. I didn't want to hurt Cara's feelings. She was so set on me adopting Harry. But I had a cat that looked a lot like this one as a child. So if you don't mind, I'd like to have Oreo."

He grinned. "I don't mind at all."

Before Sabrina left, with Oreo happily tucked into a cat crate, she had helped Garrison pick out a nice, pale robin's-egg blue for the downstairs bath and a lighter shade of gray for the downstairs bedroom. She even made some great suggestions for the bath and bedrooms upstairs.

After a quick trip to the paint store, Garrison returned with the living room and bathroom paint. He'd arranged to pick up the other cans at the end of the day and had grabbed a couple of Subway sandwiches. He and Elliott had a quick lunch, then launched into painting. "You're really good at this," he told Elliott as he watched him dipping a roller into the paint. "Have you done it before?"

Elliott flashed him a surprising grin. "Yeah, as a matter of fact."

Garrison laughed. "Well, who knew I was hiring a pro."

"I never did it as a real job," Elliott said as he rolled the paint-filled roller down the wall. "But I did help a friend paint his house last summer. I worked for free rent. It was a pretty good deal . . . at first."

"Yeah, I guess that happens sometimes," Garrison said as he used a brush to paint around the front window. "Sometimes things seem good at first . . . but we learn the hard way that they weren't as good as we thought."

"Yeah. My grandmother's always telling me that I get most of my education at the school of hard knocks. I guess she's kinda right."

"You have to decide when you're ready to quit that school," Garrison said as he dipped his brush. "Then it's time to take your life by the horns and turn it in the direction you really want to go."

"Yeah, well, that might be easier said than done."

"I know," Garrison agreed. "And I think it helps when you have someone to go alongside you. It's rough going it alone."

"You got that right."

"Hello?" called a feminine voice from the kitchen. "Anybody home?"

"We're in here," Garrison called back.

"It's just me." Beth emerged from the kitchen. "Sorry to just barge in. I came in the back door." She giggled. "I left you a little something in the kitchen."

"Really?" Garrison climbed down from the stepladder he'd been using.

"Yes. A thank-you for giving us the cat." She grinned. "Cinnamon rolls."

"Cinnamon rolls?" He smacked his lips as he removed the particle mask. "You hear that, Elliott?" He took a moment to introduce Beth to his young helper.

"I just wanted to express my thanks for giving us Spooky," Beth gushed. "You wouldn't believe the change that cat has brought to my Annabelle. It's the most remarkable thing I've ever seen. Annabelle had been so moody and distant lately. I was worried that she and I were never going to have a normal conversation again. But it's like that cat brought some kind of miracle over her." Beth paused to look around the room. "Hey, what's going on here?"

"Just fixing the place up."

"I like that color." She nodded with approval. "Where's your furniture? In storage?"

"No. I don't really have furniture. Other than a few pieces I saved from my grandmother's stuff."

"No furniture?" She got a thoughtful look. "How would you like some?"

"Huh?"

She laughed. "Well, it's a long story. You see, after my divorce—I got everything just like I deserved—but I ended up losing my big house over on Sheridan Heights just the same. That's when Annabelle and I moved over here. Anyway, with the downsize and all, the furniture from my old basement wouldn't fit. It's good stuff though, so I put it in storage, thinking maybe I'd get a real salon someday and use it in there. I thought it'd look nice in the waiting area. But that's just not happening."

"Uh-huh?" He tried to appear more interested than he felt. Beth's chatter reminded him a bit of Muzzy. Only Beth was a little more upbeat.

"So, anyway, I've been paying for this storage unit ever since we moved. Just throwing money away. I held on to the furnishings thinking I could use them in my salon—not like that's going to happen anytime soon. Then I thought maybe I'd let my ex take them. After all, he picked them out. I thought I might use them to coerce him into paying child support, but the jerk is just a deadbeat loser. And I refuse to hand them over to him now. If it wasn't the middle of winter I'd set them in my front yard and sell them."

"There are online classifieds," he suggested.

"I don't have time for that. Besides, I don't even know how." She rubbed a long red fingernail beneath her chin. "But what if . . . what if I plunked them down here for a while?"

"Here?"

"It would look fabulous, Garrison. It really would."

"But I can't afford to buy anything right now."

"Well, maybe you could in time. And if not, maybe I could just sell it when summer comes. In the meantime you'll be saving me rent money and you'd have something to sit on." She smiled hopefully.

He shrugged. "Well, when you put it like that."

Suddenly she was writing down an address and some numbers and fishing out a key. "Pick it up as soon as you can, Garrison. The payment is due on the fifteenth and I'd really like to save that rent. I could get Annabelle something nice for Christmas."

"Okay." He pocketed the slip of paper. "I'll do that. Thanks!"

"Thank *you*." She was beaming now. "And thank you for Spooky. I know that cat's the reason that Annabelle has started talking to me more. She seems so much happier. I can't even explain it. Except that I'm so grateful—for everything." She threw her arms around him, planting a big kiss on his cheek. "Thanks!" She stepped back. "And I thought the cinnamon rolls might help too."

He sniffed the air. "I can smell them."

"They're yummy. Now I gotta run. I've got a two o'clock perm."

"Thanks again," he called as she went out the back door. But before she was even gone, there was someone knocking on the front door. "This place has turned into Grand Central Station," he told Elliott as he went to answer it. "Cara?" He smiled big as he opened the door wide. "Come on in."

"Was that Beth I just saw in here?" She looked at him with a furrowed brow.

"Yeah. She brought some cinnamon rolls. Want one?"

"No . . . thanks." She turned to the wall Elliott was working on. "Nice color."

"Yeah. Sabrina picked it out. You were right, she's got a good eye for color."

"Speaking of Sabrina, I heard the news."

"News?"

"She took Oreo instead of Harry."

He shrugged. "Yeah, well, she—"

"Did you talk her out of Harry?"

"No, not at all."

"Seriously? Because I got to thinking that maybe you were saving Harry for yourself." She tilted her head to one side with a slightly suspicious expression.

"I'll admit I've gotten fond of him." He smiled. "He's a good cat."

She pointed to the face mask still in his hand. "How are your allergies?"

"As long as I stay on the meds—and after cleaning out most of the cat hair stuff—they've gotten a little better."

"That's great. So are you keeping Harry then?"

"I—uh—I don't really know."

"Oh . . . ?" She narrowed her eyes slightly, as if adding him up.

"I guess I'm still trying to figure things out." He shrugged, trying to think of a way to prolong this encounter. But it was pointless—Cara abruptly announced she had to get back to work. After she left, Garrison and Elliott sampled the cinnamon rolls and then returned to painting. But as he painted, he wondered—was Cara more interested in Harry or in him? And what about her attentive neighbor? Garrison was fully aware that David had his eye on Cara. And why shouldn't he? But how did Cara feel about David? Garrison wished he knew. What he did know was that—based on personal experience—his skills at reading women were shaky at best. And making assumptions could get a guy into trouble.

10

By Tuesday afternoon, Garrison and Elliott had finished the painting in the downstairs. They'd also removed the nasty wall-to-wall carpeting to reveal some fairly decent oak floors. "Are you going to refinish them?" Vincent asked as he kneeled down to examine the grain. He'd come by to help with some plumbing questions and was just getting ready to go.

"I don't think so," Garrison told him. "They seem okay to me."

"Yeah." Vincent stood. "If it ain't broke, why fix it."

"Especially with so much else to do," Garrison told him. "Thanks for getting that bathroom running."

"No problem. And I showed Elliott a couple of tricks so when it's time to work on the upstairs one, he might know what to do. That kid's got a good head on his shoulders."

Garrison looked outside to where Elliott was still heaping the carpet into the Dumpster. "And strong too," he said.

"But he seems troubled."

Garrison nodded, confiding in the older gentleman about how he had dreamed of creating a halfway house. "For guys just like Elliott. To help them find their way in the world." He pointed at Vincent. "They need guys like you . . . to sort of mentor them."

Vincent pointed back at Garrison. "And guys like you too. Hey, why not use this place for something like that?"

"I've considered it," Garrison admitted. "But it'd take some start-up money, which I don't have. That's why I need to take that job in Seattle."

Vincent frowned. "It'll be a shame to see you go, son."

"Yeah . . . well, I keep going back and forth on it. Who knows?" He thought about Cara. If only he could figure her out. "Maybe I'll stick around."

On Wednesday morning, Garrison rented a small moving van for half a day. "Come on," he called to Elliott as he was masking the wall along the stairway. "We've got some furniture hauling to do."

It took three trips to get the pieces moved to his house, but eventually they were put into place. A long black leather couch against the wall and two charcoal-gray leather chairs across from it. "That is sick," Elliott said as they stepped back to look at it.

"Sick?" Garrison frowned. "I think it looks cool."

Elliott laughed. "Sick *is* cool, man. Where you been?"

"In Africa?"

Elliott laughed even louder. But Garrison was encouraged to see him looking happy. The kid had a great smile. "Well, since you lived in Africa, maybe you'd like to see the rug we left outside."

"Huh?"

"I took a peek." Elliott chuckled. "It's *zebra*."

"Zebra?"

Before long they had the large rug laid out in front of the couch. "What do you think?" Garrison asked Elliott.

"Sick." Elliott's chin bobbed up and down. *"For sure."*

Garrison was not so sure. "Well, it does warm the place up a little."

Elliott pointed at Harry, who was just making himself comfortable in a sunny spot. "He likes it. But then he kinda looks like a wild animal too."

Soon they had the metal-and-glass coffee table in place, as well as a tall, dark bookshelf and some end tables. "Not bad," Garrison said as they both flopped down onto the chairs.

"Comfy too." Elliott patted the armrest. "A man could get used to this."

Garrison thought about Beth's ex. Had he gotten used to it? And, if so, would he show up and want it all back? Not that it mattered really. "Okay, let's get back to work," he told Elliott. "You see if you can finish that stairway wall and I'll return the truck."

Toward the end of the workday Garrison started working on the second-floor rooms, sorting through stuff and getting them ready for paint. As he was emptying a spare-room closet, he discovered some boxes containing artifacts from his grandparents' time spent in Africa. There were shiny black carved wooden statuettes. Spears and knives, ceremonial masks and baskets and woven mats. All sorts of interesting things that he thought might look good on that big shelf in his living room. He was just carrying them down when his cell phone rang. It was about the seventh time it had rung today. Once again, it was about the classified ad for the cats. He'd done too good a job on it and suddenly everyone was in desperate need of a cat. He gave the man the same message he'd been giving all morning. "I'm sorry, all the cats have found homes, well, except for one. And I'm considering keeping that one myself." Then, despite the man's pleas, he told him he was busy and had to go.

"I think you could've given away Harry about ten times today alone," Elliott said as Garrison walked past him with a box of artifacts. "I thought you were allergic to cats and wanted them all gone. Why you holding on to him?"

"Because I *like* him." Garrison turned off his phone. "And I'm getting sick and tired of these calls. And I mean *sick*-sick. Not sick-cool. From now on, don't call me, I'll call you," he said to his phone as he tossed it to the couch.

Elliott watched with interest, asking questions, as Garrison started to arrange the artifacts on the big shelf. Garrison, to the best of his ability, began to describe what the pieces were for, telling Elliott a bit about his time in Uganda.

"That's pretty cool what you did over there," Elliott said as he set a ceremonial knife onto the shelf. "My grandmother told me about how you put in wells so the poor people could have clean drinking water."

"Yeah. It took a whole team. I didn't do it single-handedly."

"I figured that much. But the thing is, *you did it*. You weren't that much older than me when you went over there. That was pretty unselfish, you know?"

He shrugged. "I suppose it could look that way. Truth was I wanted to go. Wanted to see the world. And I wanted to please my grandmother. All that could be considered selfish . . . depending on your perspective."

"From my perspective it looks unselfish."

Garrison looked into Elliott's eyes. "You are always surprising me."

"Huh?"

Garrison tapped Elliott's forehead. "How smart you are. How come you haven't gone to college?"

Elliott laughed. "You mean besides HKU."

"What?"

"Hard Knocks University."

"Oh yeah."

By the time Elliott went home, Garrison was exhausted. He knew it was partly because he was trying to keep up with Elliott and partly because he was gnawing on something in his mind. As foolish as it seemed, he was really considering letting the Seattle job go. What if he stuck around here and tried to turn Gram's place into a halfway house? Would it work? Or would he regret it—finding out he'd bitten off more than he could chew? Harry jumped into his lap as he sat in the living room pondering these things. "What do you think, old boy? What would you do if you were in my shoes?"

Harry gave him that adoring look—the look that clearly said he wanted Garrison to stick around and be his owner. Garrison laughed. "Yes, of course, that's because I'm currently feeding you and petting you. If someone else came along to take my place, you'd fall in love with them too."

On Thursday afternoon, Cara stopped by again. "I made too much zucchini bread," she told him as she handed over a foil-wrapped loaf that still felt warm. "I thought maybe you could use some."

"Thank you. Can you come in?"

"Well, I was just taking my afternoon walk."

"Want any company?" He brushed the dust from his hands onto his jeans.

She glanced over his shoulder. "I hate to drag you away from your work."

"No problem. Elliott's in charge anyway." He called out to Elliott. "I'll be back in a little."

"Looks like you're making progress," she said as he closed the door.

"Oh, yeah, I should've given you the full tour. It's really coming along."

"Well, it'll be dusky soon. We better walk while we've still got some light."

"Yeah . . . I still forget how night comes so much earlier in the winter. Uganda wasn't like that."

As they walked she asked him about his time in Uganda. He started by giving his usual answers, explaining about the well projects, describing the people. But then as she pressed him harder, he talked more about himself. "I get tired of people acting like I was some kind of superhero to go over there," he confessed. "There were a lot of times when I hated being there. A lot of times I felt really sorry for myself."

"That's understandable. I mean, you were there nine years."

He nodded. "And most of the time I really loved it. It was the adventure of a lifetime. I still miss it."

"Why did you come back?"

He told her about contracting malaria. "It was really my own fault. I got slack about the anti-malarial medicine. It happens a lot. When people stay there for more than a year or two, they start thinking they're invincible." He laughed sadly. "Unfortunately, it only takes a tiny mosquito to remind them otherwise."

"So that's why you came back? The malaria?"

"Yeah. It got pretty bad. They sent me home for medical help. Probably a good thing."

"And you can't go back?"

"Not anytime soon." He told her about his more recent dreams, about creating a halfway house, and even a bit about Elliott. "It's really giving me hope."

"Do you think you might stay here? Make a halfway house in your grandmother's house?"

"I'm seriously considering it." He confessed to how lost he had felt these past few months. "It was like I couldn't find my way. Couldn't get my feet beneath me," he told her as the sky grew duskier. Something about this purple-gray light made him feel more comfortable talking about his feelings. It was kind of like being in a confessional—where you couldn't see a priest. Not that he was Catholic or had ever done that, but he could imagine. "I felt like I was an old man, all washed up at the ripe old age of thirty-four."

"I'm thirty-two," she said quietly. "I can't imagine feeling washed up in a couple of years."

"Well, that's how I felt. Like my best life was behind me. Like I gave all I had and had lost a lot of myself in the process." Or maybe he'd just never known himself to start with.

"How could you lose yourself?"

He shrugged. "Maybe it was my heart that I lost while I was over there."

"Your heart?" she said quietly.

"There was a girl that I thought I was in love with." He

sighed, wishing he hadn't mentioned this. But there it was—out there. His admission to failure in the romance arena.

"Oh?"

"Yeah. Her name was Leah and I was pretty sure that the sun and the moon rose because of her." He made a forced laugh. "For a while she even pretended to care for me."

"Pretended?"

"Yeah . . . I'm pretty sure it was an act. Turned out she had another guy on the line the whole while she was spending time with me. I think she actually used me to make him jealous. Anyway, they are happily married now. With a baby too. Really, I wish them no ill. But it did hurt. It took its toll."

"Yeah . . . I can imagine."

"But here's the deal," he said suddenly. "I'm starting to feel found again. Like I really am coming back to life. I know it's partly due to feeling healthier now. The malaria is under control. But there's something about being here. Something about working on Gram's house. Spending time with Elliott. Even hanging with Harry . . . it all feels *right*." He paused under the streetlight, turning to smile at her. She smiled back and suddenly he longed to take her hand in his. He wanted to tell her that she was a big part of the "rightness" that was happening in his life. But at the same time, he didn't want to scare her off. Already, he'd said much more than he'd intended.

Instead of making what could turn into an awkward declaration, and since it was now dark, he insisted on walking her home. As they walked down her street, he lightened the conversation by telling her more about Elliott and how he recognized some great potential in the young man. "Here we are," he said as they walked up to her door.

"But now I'll miss seeing the improvements in your house," she declared as they stood on the front porch together.

"Come by tomorrow," he told her. "I'll give you the full tour. I promise."

As he walked home, he wondered if he'd been presumptuous to escort her all the way up to her door. As if he'd thought they were on a date. The last thing he wanted was to overwhelm her. Especially considering how they'd gotten off on the wrong foot over Harry last week. And he knew that his dating skills, at best, were rusty. He needed to go carefully with this woman . . . pace himself. Just the same, his step lightened as he considered the progress they'd made this evening. And he would get to see her again tomorrow!

On Friday morning, as Garrison worked on the second-floor rooms, he got an idea. Rather, Harry gave him an idea. It seemed that whichever room Garrison was working on, Harry was determined to occupy. But as Garrison was talking to the cat, telling him to keep his tail out of the paint tray, it hit him. If he kept Harry, why couldn't he keep the ten grand that was supposed to go with Harry? Wouldn't that be fair? Or would Gram's attorney have objections because he didn't meet Gram's strict requirements? But that seemed ridiculous. After all, he was her grandson. Wouldn't she be delighted he'd gotten over his cat phobia and wanted one of her cats?

With that ten grand, Garrison could afford to pass on the Seattle job. He could buy himself time to figure things out here. Perhaps he could even start up the halfway house.

Maybe he could get the church to back him. After all, they had backed him with Uganda. Suddenly it all seemed very doable.

He went to search for his phone, turning it on to see there were even more messages now. It seemed everyone wanted a cat now. Ignoring the messages, he called Mr. Miller, but discovering he was out of town until Monday, he told the assistant he'd call back. But even as he turned off his phone again, he felt hopeful. This plan could work! However, he knew better than to call Seattle and burn that bridge. It had taken far too long to land that job. No way was he going to toss it aside without some kind of assurance from Mr. Miller.

The bulk of the work in the house was pretty much wrapped up by noon, and to celebrate, Garrison ordered pizza for Vincent and Elliott. "You guys are the best," Garrison said as he held up a slice of pizza like a toast. "I never would've accomplished all this without your help."

"I've enjoyed having a project to dig into," Vincent admitted. "Wish I could do some of these upgrades in my own house."

"Well, when your ship comes in and you're ready to do some renovations, don't forget that I owe you," Garrison told him. He wanted to add that, come Christmas Eve, Vincent would have some unexpected cash to work with.

"I'll remember that," Vincent said a bit doubtfully. "When my ship comes in." He pointed at Elliott. "And if that should happen, I'd like to hire you, young man. The three of us could really do some great things on my house."

"Just let me know," Elliott said as he reached for another slice.

They talked and joked about the work they'd done and Garrison could tell they were all a little sad to see it coming to an end. "But don't forget," he reminded them, "as soon as the weather starts warming up, I'll want to start working on the exterior of the house. We'll have a reunion tour in the spring."

The doorbell rang as they were cleaning up the pizza mess. As Garrison went to answer it, Vincent excused himself, and Elliott said he was going upstairs to put a final coat of paint on the bathroom baseboard.

Cara was at the door, smiling expectantly. "Is this an okay time for a tour?"

"Perfect." He welcomed her in, explaining how they were just finishing up. Then he led her around the house, taking her from room to room while she gushed over the progress he'd made.

"I never could've done it without Elliott and Vincent," he said. "We made a pretty great team."

"Well, you've really turned this house around," she declared as they came back to the living room.

"There are still lots of little things to do," he said. "But the big stuff is done."

"And you even have furniture." She made a puzzled frown as she sat on the leather couch. "Very manly too."

He laughed. "That's just temporary. Beth's ex-husband picked it out." He explained about the storage unit.

"Oh . . . so you're kind of storing it for her?"

"Something like that." He grinned. "Although Elliott thinks it's *sick*."

She smiled. "As in cool, right?"

"Yeah. You knew that already?"

She laughed. "Unlike some people I haven't been living under a rock."

He feigned a wounded expression. Unfortunately, she was right.

"Sorry," she said quickly. "I didn't mean—"

"No problem. Just jerking your chain." He grinned.

She laughed as she stood. "Well then, on that note, I think I should go."

"Did I scare you away?"

"No, I just have a lot to get done before quitting time."

"Speaking of quitting time . . ." He followed her to the door, trying to think of a clever way to ask her out. "I, uh, I've been meaning to invite you to dinner. I'd like to properly thank you for all your help in finding homes for the cats. Are you busy tonight?"

"I'm sorry," she said as she opened the door. "I, uh, I already have plans."

Garrison just nodded, trying to determine if this was her way of saying he'd just stepped over the line. "Yeah . . . well, that's okay." He shoved his hands into his pockets, trying to act nonchalant. But for some reason this felt like a brush-off. Like Cara was being insincere . . . just making an excuse not to go out with him. He followed her out to the porch—more to be polite than because he wanted to.

"Okay, I can tell you don't believe me," she said a bit contritely.

He shrugged. "Hey, if you don't want to go out with me, I understand. I'd just like to think you'd be honest with me." He looked directly into her eyes. "We are friends, *right*?"

"Of course," she declared. "But I am being honest. I really do have a previous engagement tonight. I promised David that I'd go to a Christmas party with him and there's—"

"Cara, you don't have to report to me," he said too abruptly. "I *said* I understand. No big deal. I get it."

"Well, okay then." She let out a frustrated sigh and he

knew that he'd hurt her, but how could he take it back? "I better go," she said quietly.

"Yeah . . . me too." As he went back inside, Garrison knew he was being immature. He knew that this wasn't how you treated people—friend or not. But hearing that Cara had a date with David—well, that just cut him to the core. Especially after some of the things he'd shared with her. Sure, he was being juvenile, but he just couldn't seem to help himself. As he continued washing paintbrushes in the laundry sink, he tried not to think about it. But in his mind's eye he kept seeing them together. Cara in her garnet-red knit dress or maybe even something more alluring. David in a suave dark suit. Together . . . laughing . . . dancing . . . falling in love.

"Hey, man, are you painting or cleaning brushes?" Elliott asked as he stuck his head in the laundry room.

Garrison forced a smile. "Caught me."

"Well, I gotta go. Promised my grandmother we'd take in a flick tonight." He made a face. "Hope I don't see anyone I know."

"If you do, just hold your head high. Show them that you're man enough to be seen in public with your grandmother. If they don't respect you, they don't deserve your respect."

Elliott nodded. "Yeah, man, I think you're right."

The next morning, despite feeling a bit like Scrooge, Garrison decided to take in the Christmas parade. As he walked to town, he remembered the last time he'd been here for a Christmas parade. He'd been playing trombone in the high school marching band and hoping to catch the eye of a pretty majorette named Jenny—who probably still didn't know his name. Had things really changed much since then?

As he turned his collar up against the morning chill, he decided a Christmas parade was just the ticket to cheer him up. On his way, he strolled past the staging area, looking on with amusement as he passed the homemade floats and marching band members tuning their instruments and trying not to appear nervous. He grinned at a group of costumed children from the school of dance, stomping their feet to stay warm. Everyone was anxiously awaiting the firehouse whistle to signal it was time to begin.

Feeling unexplainably giddy himself, he hurried past the staging area and on toward Main Street. Eager to find a good spot where he could watch the small-town spectacle, he wondered how he'd managed to celebrate Christmas all these years without a folksy parade to kick it off.

He was just going past the hardware store when he spied Cara. It wasn't exactly like he was looking for her, but it wasn't exactly like he wasn't. Plus she was easy to spot. Her bright red scarf wrapped carelessly around her neck seemed to set off her shining chestnut hair. "Hey, Cara," he said as he stepped up next to her.

"Garrison!" Her eyes sparkled with surprise—or perhaps pleasure?

Garrison noticed the boy on her other side. "Hey, Jackson," he said in a friendly tone. "What's up, my man?" Okay, he sounded like a bad imitation of Elliott, but he was only trying to be friendly . . . to fit in.

Jackson flashed him a crooked smile. "Not much."

"How's Muzzy doing?" Garrison asked, hoping to encourage the boy to engage like his dad wanted him to.

"She's fine." Jackson nodded eagerly. "She's a *good* cat."

"Is she talking your ear off yet?"

Jackson laughed. "Yeah."

"Garrison!" David exclaimed as he joined them. "How's it going?"

"Pretty good," Garrison said with a stiff smile. "How about you?"

"I'm great. Thanks." David, wearing a black fedora and walking coat, resembled an ad for a fashion magazine. In his gloved hands was a cardboard tray with three hot drinks balanced in it. But he was gazing intently at Garrison as if he was in the way somehow.

Garrison got it. Barely nodding, he stepped away from Cara's side. Like clockwork, David slid right into the same spot—like he belonged there. And maybe he did. Clearly the three of them had come together to watch the parade. In fact, they actually looked like a family. Even though he was obviously odd man out, Garrison stubbornly remained in place. Sure, he could admit it—at least to himself: he was as socially challenged as young Jackson.

David's blue eyes twinkled as he handed a cup to Cara. "Here you go, my lady. Your mocha—just how you like it—dash of cinnamon, splash of vanilla."

"Thanks," she murmured with downcast eyes. Was she playing the coquette or was she simply embarrassed by David's patronizing and somewhat territorial attention? And really, why was Garrison remaining stubbornly in place? It was clear that his presence wasn't welcome.

"And here's your cocoa, bud." David handed his son a cup, giving Garrison an apologetic look. "If I'd known you were here, old man, I'd have got you a coffee too."

"No problem." Garrison forced a smile. "I was just about to head over to the coffee shop myself."

David held out the cardboard tray to him. "Hey, then maybe you can take this back for me. Recycling—good for the earth you know." He grinned victoriously.

Garrison took the tray and, feeling dismissed, said a quick goodbye and continued on his way. He wanted to throw the tray to the ground and smash it beneath his boot, but he knew that would make him look like a jealous fool. Already he felt stupid enough. What difference should it make to him if Cara wanted to watch the parade with her neighbors? Why shouldn't she?

Garrison picked up a newspaper, then got in line for coffee, telling himself that the mature thing was to grab his beverage then go back and enjoy the Christmas festivities with the three of them. After all, they were neighbors—right?

But as he ordered his coffee he heard the firehouse whistle blow and by the time his coffee was ready, the parade was well on its way. Instead of going out to the street to watch it, he sat down at a small table by the window and watched the parade—by himself. He felt like the kid with his nose pressed against the toy store window—longing for something he could never have—hoping for Santa to do the impossible, yet knowing that Santa wasn't real.

Garrison knew he looked pathetic sitting there by himself, moping over his coffee while pretending to peruse the local paper, but it was the best he could manage. Why had he let Cara get under his skin like this? Hadn't he learned his lesson with Leah in Uganda? Would he ever learn?

The best thing to do is get on with your life, he chided himself. Quit moping around and wrap up Gram's business and get himself back to Seattle where a job—and who knew what else—awaited him. He pulled out his phone and, for the first time in days, turned it on. To his surprise there were thirty-three messages—and all from strange local numbers. That silly ad had really done the trick. Garrison had no doubt what these people wanted. He listened to a few of them just to confirm his suspicions. All of them were eager to adopt a cat—unexplainably eager. Yet the more pleas he listened to, the more he wanted to keep Harry for himself.

But he knew that was crazy and selfish. Harry would not be happy in Randall's apartment—left alone all day while Garrison was at work and stuck in a small apartment with no access to the outdoors. That wasn't fair or kind. And Gram would never have approved. Besides that, what about his allergies? Did he want to continue taking allergy meds nonstop around the clock? Did he want to be forced to wear particle masks?

He knew it wasn't just selfish to keep Harry for himself, it was plain wrong. Harry was a good cat. He deserved better. But if he had to part with Harry, he was determined to find him a really good home. As he walked back to Gram's house, he began responding to the messages, sifting through and eliminating the callers. For the first time he was really thankful for Gram's list.

By the time Garrison got home from the parade, he knew what had to be done. Even if it wasn't easy, it was the right thing to do. He solemnly dialed the Maxwells' number, inwardly hoping no one would answer.

"I'm so glad you called," Mr. Maxwell said after Garrison went over the usual preliminaries. "We lost a beloved family dog a few months ago. My children were completely devastated. I'm still getting over it myself. I never knew that an animal could steal my heart like Barnie did. So much so that I told myself I'd never get another pet." He made a loud sigh. "But my children don't agree. So I thought . . . why not get a cat?"

"Well, this is a very special cat," Garrison told him. "Almost like a dog."

"That sounds like my kind of cat."

"So . . ." Garrison stroked Harry's thick coat as they sat together on the sofa. "The only thing left is the home visit."

"Yeah, sure," the man said eagerly. "Anytime you want. My wife and kids are out right now. Christmas shopping. But I'm here . . . just watching the Steelers game."

Garrison looked out the window where, despite the cold temperature, the sun was shining. Gently sliding Harry off his lap, he slowly stood. "I'll be there in about ten minutes." Grabbing up his coat, he hurried out the door, hoping that the short walk to the address he'd just been given would help clear his head and remind him, once again, why Harry needed to be placed in a "real" home. It wasn't fair for him to try to hold on to Harry. In fact, it was just plain selfish. And he knew it.

The Maxwells' home was a well-maintained but modest ranch-style house. Mr. Maxwell, wearing jeans and a Steelers sweatshirt, answered the door with a big grin and introduced himself as Tom. He tipped his head into the house. "Come on in. Feel free to look around. Make yourself at home."

It didn't take long for Garrison to see that there was nothing wrong with what was obviously a family home. Personality seemed to ooze from every space. In some ways it seemed like the American dream—mom and dad and three kids. All they needed was a dog—or a cat. Garrison told Mr. Maxwell that he'd passed the home visit.

"But you'd probably like to meet Harry first," he said. "I mean, cats do have personalities and temperaments, and although Harry is the sweetest cat I've ever known, you can never tell whether it will work. You guys might not be compatible." Garrison felt silly for talking about a cat like it was a human. But in some ways Harry felt human. And lately he'd been Garrison's best friend.

"Okay. Let me record this game and I'll drive you home. Then if Harry and I hit it off, maybe I can bring him back with me. It'd be a great surprise for the wife and kids when they get home."

Garrison agreed and it wasn't long until he was enticing Harry into the last cat crate. But the look in Harry's eyes nearly broke Garrison's heart. It was as if Harry knew, as if he were saying, "How could you? I thought you loved me. I thought we were buddies. Don't you want me anymore? What did I do wrong?"

"See you around, pal," Garrison said with a husky voice, closing the door of the crate and latching it with a finality that broke his heart. Suppressing the stinging tears that were building in the back of his eyes, he handed the crate over to Tom. "Take good care of him. I'll be by to visit in two weeks. And then another week after that."

Tom's brow furrowed. "Your grandmother must've really liked her cats, huh?"

"You got that right." Garrison literally herded Tom and Harry toward the front door, practically pushing them out. "Take care," he called out as he firmly shut the door. He leaned against it, trying to catch his breath and calm himself. But it was too late. Tears were pouring down his face and his chest ached from the pain of trying to contain them.

"*What is wrong with me?*" he shouted as he went to the bathroom to splash cold water on his face. "I'm a grown man—bawling over a stupid cat!" He looked up at his pitiful image in the bathroom mirror. "Okay," he said in an attempt to get control. "This is obviously not just about the cat. This is about loss and heartache and heartbreak . . . This is about Uganda and Leah and Gram and Cara

. . . and—and—" A guttural sob escaped his throat. *"This is about Harry too!"*

Despite its improved appearance, the house felt sad and empty and lonely. And with the landline phone unplugged and Garrison's cell phone off—to avoid the barrage of cat inquiries still coming even though he'd canceled the ad—it was as quiet as a tomb. To distract himself, Garrison focused his attention on the real estate section of the local paper. One real estate company seemed to run more ads than any other, using big colored photos and great house descriptions. Garrison turned on his phone and, selecting the photo of an agent who looked to be around sixty, dialed the number.

"This is Barb Foster," a friendly female voice answered. "What can I do for you?"

Liking her tone, Garrison quickly explained his interest in listing his house. "Maybe I shouldn't have called you on the weekend," he said apologetically. "But I just saw your ad and I thought—"

"Haven't you heard that real estate agents work seven days a week?" she said cheerfully. "In fact, we expect to work even harder on the weekends. Now, tell me more about your house, Garrison."

He explained the recent improvements he'd made. "I'm not saying the place is perfect by any means. But it's a lot better. I'd try to sell it myself, but I really don't know a thing about real estate. I did some looking in the classifieds, but I have no idea where to begin. Plus I need to get back to Seattle for my job."

"Well, darling, you've called the right person. I've been

working in real estate for more than thirty-five years. There's not much I don't know about this business." She asked him some preliminary questions and eventually inquired about the address. "That's an interesting neighborhood," she told him. "It went downhill in the late nineties, but it's been making a nice little comeback lately. I'll do some comps and come up with a number for you."

"Comps?"

"Comparing house prices. I also look at tax records and some other things. We want to price the house just right. Not too high, not too low. *Right on the money.*" She chuckled. "And that brings you the money. Do you want me to start working on it for you?"

Garrison felt drawn to the warmth in her voice. She had an almost maternal sound. "Yes," he declared. "I want to move forward." He glanced around the lonely house. "As soon as possible."

"Well, you're in luck because I'm doing an open house today and it's been pretty slow on this side of town. I've got my iPad with me, and I'll start looking into your property right now. Then if you don't mind, I'll stop by around four and take a look at your property."

"That's fine. Great!"

By the time Barb showed up, Garrison felt so unbearably lonely that he rushed to open the door and invited her in with enthusiasm. Chattering at her nonstop—similar to what Muzzy used to do—Garrison showed Barb everything.

"The place looks good," she told him. "Like you said, it's not perfect. But it's clean and cleared out." She glanced around. "Almost too cleared out."

"Really?"

"But don't worry about that."

"So do you want to list it?" he asked hopefully. "I mean, I realize the holidays are coming. Maybe that's not a good time to—"

"Oh, you'd be surprised at the people who enjoy house shopping during the holidays. Folks are visiting relatives or just driving around to look at Christmas decorations." Her eyes lit up. "Say, we should put some nice, tasteful lights outside—really show the place off. And we should put a tree up and add a few Christmas touches." She pointed to the mantel. "Maybe some greens and candles and such."

He gave her a blank look. "I—uh—to be honest, I'm not really good at that sort of thing."

She laughed. "No, of course not." She pointed to the zebra rug. "Clearly this is a bachelor pad. But that's not what buyers want to see. Let me take care of that for you. You've done a great job already, darling, but we need to warm it up. My daughter-in-law is a magician at staging."

"Staging?"

Barb explained how houses sold more easily when the furnishings were arranged in a certain way. "Felicia will bring some things over—just on loan until your house sells. She'll get the place looking like something right out of a magazine."

"Really?"

"You bet. Like I said, this girl is a whiz. My guess is we'll have this place sold before the new year. How does that work for you?"

He forced a smile, realizing this was really it—the end of an era. It felt like a large stone had lodged itself in the bottom of his stomach. "Uh—yeah, sure. That sounds great."

She patted his hand. "I understand, son. This was your

grandmother's house, your childhood home. It's only natural you should feel some sadness."

He nodded. "Yeah, it's hard to give it up. But at the same time, I know it would be harder to stay." He looked around. "It's pretty lonely here."

As soon as Barb left, Garrison called Randall in Seattle, quickly explaining his job and a need to return. "Hopefully you won't be stuck with me too long," he said. "My plan is to get a place of my own as soon as possible." He told him about listing Gram's house.

"No problem," Randall said easily. *"Mi casa es su casa."*

"Thanks." Garrison let out a relieved sigh. "Can't wait to see you, bud."

After he hung up, Garrison decided to take a walk. Partly because he was restless, partly because he needed to get out of the house. It felt like the loneliness was eating him alive. The air was crisp and cold and since it was late in the day, the streets were vacant of foot traffic. Many of his neighbors' houses were lit up with strings of Christmas lights and cheerful decorations. But even the ones that weren't had the warm amber glow of lights flowing from windows, suggesting that the people inside were happily enjoying each other's company, maybe fixing meals together, sharing a laugh, watching a football game. For the second time today, he felt like the kid with his nose pressed against the window. He felt left out . . . lost, lonely, longing . . .

As the daylight faded he decided to venture over to Cara's street. Yes, he knew he might look like a stalker, but it wasn't like he was planning anything sinister. He just wanted one last look. Feeling somewhat concealed by the dusky light, he slowly strolled past Cara's house. She had put up Christmas lights too, making her sweet little home resemble a gingerbread house even more. David and Jackson's house had similar lights on it. Perhaps they had all worked together to put them up. Garrison could imagine the three of them with ladders and tangled strings of lights, laughing and drinking hot cocoa together, maybe even singing Christmas songs as they "decked their halls."

Feeling chilled to the bone, he turned the next corner and jogged back home, where the starkness of his bachelor pad greeted him like a glass of cold water tossed into his face. As he went to the kitchen to fix himself some dinner, he looked around, expecting one of his furry feline friends to appear—for Harry to rub up against his legs. Of course, that was not happening. "I've got to get out of here," he said as he opened the freezer, removing a microwavable meal. "The sooner the better."

13

"Why'd you give him away?" Elliott demanded on Sunday. "I thought you liked him—I thought you were gonna keep him?"

"I can't keep him," Garrison said for the second time. Elliott had popped in to say a friendly hello, but had grown increasingly irate after discovering that Harry had found a new home.

"Why not?"

"Because I have to get back to Seattle. My job starts—"

"You're leaving?"

"Well, yeah . . . I have to—"

"What about the halfway house? My grandmother said you might make this place into a halfway house for guys?"

"That was just a dream, Elliott. A dream that takes money."

"What about faith, man?" Elliott glared at him with dark eyes. "You been talking to me about being a man of faith? Where's your faith now?"

Garrison frowned, not wanting to admit that he hadn't even attended church this morning . . . that he'd barely been able to drag himself out of bed . . . where was the faith in that? "I still have faith," he muttered.

"Not enough faith to make this place work. You let Harry go. You just give up and leave. You're just like everyone else, man." Elliott pounded his fist onto the kitchen counter. "Well, I can leave too!"

"*Wait!*" Garrison called. "You don't understand."

But it was too late, Elliott was already storming out. And before the back door slammed shut, Garrison observed the real estate agent's car pulling into the driveway. Wearing a stylish navy pantsuit, Barb got out of her car and went around to the trunk. He watched as she removed something bulky. Of course, it was a For Sale sign. She leaned it against her car, then, carrying a packet of papers, walked up to the front door. *This is it*, he realized as he went to answer it. Now everyone in the neighborhood would know that he was leaving. Well, maybe that was just as well. The sooner they figured it out the better.

Garrison signed the agreement. Just as he finished helping Barb plant the sign in his front yard, he noticed a hefty figure wearing a purple woolen coat and a matching hat marching toward him. "That's my neighbor," he said quietly to Barb. "And she looks like she's on the warpath."

"*What?*" Barb looked up in alarm.

"I didn't tell her I was selling the place."

"Oh, well, I'll make myself scarce." She gave him a little finger wave then hurried back to her car.

"What in tarnation do you think you're doing?" Ruby demanded.

"Listen, Ruby, I wanted to tell—"

"*What are you doing?*"

"I have to go back to Seattle. I have a job there and—"

"What about your halfway house? What about Elliott?"

"It's a dream, Ruby. And sometimes dreams take time and—"

"*Yes!*" She shook her finger beneath his nose. "And you have to *give* them time, Garrison. You are not giving this enough time! You're running off like a scaredy-cat, boy. Your grandmother would be ashamed of you."

"How do you know that?" he demanded.

"Because I am ashamed of you."

"Just because I'm going to take a job in Seattle? Because I'm selling this house? Why should that make you ashamed?"

"Because it looks to me like you're giving up." She peered at him with misty-looking brown eyes. "In my heart, I feel that you just gave up. Like you let something whip you, and now you're running off with your tail tucked between your legs." She shook her head grimly. "I can't even explain it, but I just feel it inside here." She tapped her chest. "In my heart, I am sure that you are making a big mistake."

He didn't know what to say.

"What about Harry?" she asked with a smidgeon of hope in her eyes.

"I found him a home . . . yesterday." He held up his hands hopelessly. "You wouldn't believe how many people have called to adopt cats," he said quickly, hoping to change the subject. "I must have a hundred messages by now. It's uncanny."

She shrugged. "Well, that's because of the rumor."

"Rumor?"

"You haven't heard?"

"What do you mean?"

"The million-dollar-cat rumor. It's circulating around town."

"What are you talking about?"

"Somehow folks got it into their heads that one of Lilly's cats—or maybe all of them depending on who you listen to—is going to inherit a million dollars." She gave him a smirking look. "I know it's plum foolish, but that's what folks are saying. Everyone's talking about the million-dollar cat. I expect that's why you got so many calls." She gave him a suspicious look. "You did find Harry a good home, didn't you?"

Garrison nodded sadly. "Yeah. It's fine."

"Just tell me one thing," she began again. "Why can't you just stay here until Christmas?"

"Because I can't."

"Why not?" she pleaded.

"They need me on the job *now*," he said firmly. "I'm supposed to report on the tenth."

She took in a deep breath then pursed her lips. It looked like she wanted to explode all over again.

"I'm sorry, Ruby."

"I'm sorry too, Garrison. Sorry for you."

"But you'll forgive me, won't you?"

She narrowed her eyes. "As a Christian woman, I have to forgive you. But as your grandma's good friend, I do not have to like it." She turned to walk away. "No," she repeated, "I do *not* have to like it!"

After getting a new cell phone number the next morning, Garrison stopped by Mr. Miller's office, explaining his need to get to Seattle. "I promised to be on the job by the tenth and that's tomorrow. Is it okay if I do the two-week checkups today? It'll be a couple days early for some of them, but—"

"I don't think that's a problem. That is, if you feel confident you've found them all good homes."

"I honestly think I have. And if I can wrap this up, I'd really appreciate it." Then he remembered Harry. "Although one of the cats was only placed a couple days ago. That two-week check is a ways off and I'll be working in Seattle then."

"Hmm . . ." Mr. Miller wobbled a pencil back and forth between his fingers. "Maybe I could check on that one for you."

"Sure, I'd appreciate that." Garrison felt a wave of relief. The last thing he needed right now was to visit Harry and have that cat look longingly with those pale green eyes. He already missed Harry far more than he'd imagined possible. Almost as much as he missed Cara—although he was determined not to dwell on that. Onward and upward.

"The most important part of all this is the final visit. And that'll be up to you to do." Mr. Miller aimed his pencil at Garrison. "Only you can determine if the cats are properly settled—and it's your job to deliver the checks too."

"The deadline lands right before Christmas for five of the cats. Although Harry, the one I placed most recently . . . is later." Garrison frowned. "Does that mean I'll have to make a special trip from Seattle to check on him?"

"Hmm . . . I'm thinking out loud here . . . since that's the cat I'll be checking on next week, maybe we can bend the rules a little. If I decide that it's a good home, I'll recommend that you include that cat's final visit with the others. How's that sound?"

"That'd be great. That way everyone will get their bonuses before Christmas."

"Good. Now you email me your two-week report along with all the names and addresses of the new pet owners, and I'll have my assistant prepare a package for you. It'll be ready to pick up"—he paused to write this down—"on the twenty-fourth." He smiled at Garrison. "And you can have the pleasure of playing Santa Claus."

"Great."

"And just so you know I'll be leaving town on the twentieth. Taking the family on a ski vacation for Christmas. But Ellen will be here, although I told her she could leave early on Christmas Eve. So the sooner you get here, the sooner she can be on her way."

"I'll do what I can to leave work early that day," he assured him. Then they tied up a few more loose ends and, feeling satisfied that he was getting closer to having fulfilled his grandmother's final wishes, Garrison thanked the lawyer and left. Now all he needed to do was to make some quick visits to check on the cats.

He stopped by Vincent's house first. Vincent, wearing a checkered apron, was in his kitchen making cranberry-nut bread. Rusty was basking in the sunshine on a kitchen chair, watching his master it seemed.

"This is a recipe my wife liked to use," Vincent explained as he wiped his hands on the front of his apron. "I never tried it before myself, but for some reason I felt inspired today. Or maybe I was just hungry for it."

"How are you and Rusty getting along?" Garrison reached down to scratch the big orange cat's chin.

"Like a pair of old pals." Vincent grinned at the cat. "Two bachelors making the best of it."

"He appears happy and healthy." Garrison looked at

Vincent. "Also I wanted to let you know I'm heading back for Seattle this afternoon. Took the job there after all."

Vincent's smile faded. "You're leaving? So soon?"

"Yeah." He shrugged. "Gainful employment . . . so to speak."

"Well, you'll be missed around here."

Garrison nodded. "I really appreciate all the help you gave me on the house. Wish I could be around at payback time."

Vincent's brow creased. "No worries there. My finances aren't going to change."

Garrison wanted to disagree, but at the same time, he did not want to let the cat out of the bag. He smiled to himself at the appropriateness of that metaphor, then shook Vincent's hand and promised that he'd be back in time for Christmas.

Since Beth's house was only a few blocks away, he made that his next stop. Beth was in the midst of touching up an older woman's roots. Garrison, seeing that Spooky looked perfectly fine and was actually a bit more friendly than he recalled—or maybe Garrison's general opinion toward cats had changed—told Beth that he had no complaints. "Looks like Spooky has found herself a perfect home," he told her.

"I wish you could see Annabelle and Spooky together," Beth told him as he pulled his coat back on. "It's like they were made for each other." She smiled. "Thank you again!"

He told her about his house being on the market. "So if it sells, we'll have to figure out what to do with your furniture."

She waved her hand. "Who knows? Maybe the buyers will want to purchase the furnishings too. I wouldn't argue with that."

He told her he'd mention that to his agent, then promised to be back in touch shortly before Christmas.

Next he went to Riley and Sabrina's house to check on Oreo. He had no doubts that Oreo would be in good shape and, after Sabrina let him into the house, he knew the cat had fallen into a sweet little nest. "I just love him," she told Garrison as she cuddled the cat in her arms. "I don't know why I didn't think to get a cat ages ago." She rubbed her face into his. "Although I'm glad I waited for this one. He's really a darling."

Once again, Garrison made the speech about returning to do the final check at Christmastime, but before he got out the door, Sabrina stopped him. "I know it's none of my business," she said in a careful tone. "But I'm curious about what went wrong with you and Cara."

He gave her a puzzled look. "What do you mean?"

She shrugged. "I don't know . . . you guys just seemed like a good pair."

"Well . . . I . . . uh . . . I'm not sure what you're getting at."

"I just wondered what came between you two."

He frowned. "I guess it was David."

Her brows arched and he excused himself. "See you around Christmas," he called as he hurried out.

As he drove around the block to David's house he was curious. Why had Sabrina said that? Did she know something he didn't? And, if so, what was it? Glancing at Cara's house, he noticed the car missing from her driveway, then remembered how she worked in the city on Mondays. Probably for the best.

He tried to bury any resentment he felt toward David as he knocked on the door. This was not about Garrison—this was about a cat. Muzzy, to be specific. David was perfectly courteous and, once again, Garrison felt completely reassured that another cat had landed in the perfect home. Perfect for Muzzy and perfect for Jackson. And, unless Garrison was imagining things, Jackson's social skills were improving too. He thanked David and reminded him that he'd do the final check right before Christmas. As he got back into his car, he did not allow his eyes to wander over to the gingerbread house. Best not to look back.

The last one on his list was Viola, although he knew there was really no reason to check on that cat. She was perfectly happy with Ruby. However, he wanted a second chance to make things right with one of Gram's dearest friends—a woman who'd been like an aunt to him. But before he knocked on her back door, he made one last check on the house and put his bags into the back of the Pontiac. His plan was to be on the road by two.

Ruby scowled darkly as she let him into her kitchen. "I s'pose you're here to check on Viola," she said in a grumpy voice. "As if I don't know how to take care of my own cat by now."

"I had no doubts about that," he assured her. "I was more interested in seeing you. I'm sorry to find you in such bad spirits. Are you still mad at me?"

She rolled her eyes. "The world does not turn around you, Garrison Brown."

He blinked. "No, I didn't think it did."

"If you must know, I'm out of sorts over Elliott."

"Elliott? What's he done?"

"He's done left."

"Left?"

"That's right. Took off in the middle of the night. Not so much as a fare-thee-well from that ungrateful boy's lips."

"Ruby . . . I'm sorry." He put a hand on her shoulder.

"Oh, Garrison." She broke into sobs and he wrapped his arms around her. "I had such hopes for that boy. Seemed like he was really connecting with you."

"I'm sorry, Ruby." His voice choked. "I feel this is partly my fault."

She stepped back, fishing a tissue from her sleeve and wiping her nose. "No, no, that's not fair. I'm not blaming you for my grandson's bad choices." She looked intently into his eyes. "You are only responsible for your own bad choices, boy."

He nodded glumly. "That's true."

"You see to it that you don't make any more bad choices—you hear Ruby now?"

"Yes. I hear." He kissed her cheek. "And you and Viola take care. I'll see you at Christmas."

She brightened a little. "Oh yeah, that's right—you bringing me my million dollars to go with that cat, right?" She laughed like she knew that was never happening.

"I wish I could do that," he told her. "I'm sure you'd put it to good use."

Her chin bobbed up and down with strength. "You got that right. First of all I'd buy that house next door and turn it into a halfway house."

He grinned. "I'll bet you would."

As they hugged again, he promised to pray for Elliott and she promised to fix him another chicken pot pie the next time he came home. And then he got into the Pontiac and headed north to Seattle.

14

There had been a time when Garrison had loved being in Seattle. The photogenic landscape of mountains and water and sky had never failed to energize him, and the beat of the city had always filled him with enthusiasm and high expectations. But something had changed . . . and he didn't think it was Seattle.

To be fair, the grim, gray weather was not helping any. But Garrison tried to remain focused on his new job, his new boss, and the possibility of moving into a new apartment—when Gram's house sold. According to Barb, it could happen any day now.

"My first open house was a huge success," she'd told him shortly after he'd returned to Seattle. "I ran it on both Saturday and Sunday. And I had more than thirty people go through."

"Thirty?"

"Well, certainly some of them were Looky-Lous and some were just your curious neighbors wanting to see what you'd done with the place. But there were at least two families who were seriously shopping for a home. And, oh my, you should see how fabulous Felicia has made your house look. You probably wouldn't recognize it. I've got all the real estate agents in town coming through on Thursday. I wouldn't be surprised if we got an offer even before Christmas."

"Really?" He felt a mixture of anxiety and hope. On one hand, he wasn't ready to let go . . . on the other hand he had no choice.

By the end of his second week back in Seattle, Garrison felt so blue that he wondered if he was coming down with something. Or maybe his malaria was flaring up. But his temperature registered normal. And besides feeling gloomy and weary, he had no real symptoms. Telling himself it was simply the cold, wet weather getting him down, he jogged through the company parking lot and jumped into the Pontiac. Within minutes he was headed down the freeway. His hope was to reach the Miller law firm before three o'clock to pick up the packet. He knew that Mr. Miller had been out of the office most of the week and that his assistant planned to close early. Garrison had promised to get there before she locked up.

As he drove south, he tried not to think of what kind of a Christmas he would have this year—certainly not a traditional one. But, to be fair, his past nine Christmases in Uganda had not been traditional either. Yet they had been sweet . . . and genuine . . . filled with good-hearted people.

He turned the radio on, tuning to a station that was playing nothing but Christmas songs, and before long he started feeling cheery. After all, he was about to play Santa Claus in a very real sort of way. Handing out sizeable checks to some very decent folks—what could be better? He tried to imagine their surprised faces. Hopefully they'd be surprised. He remembered the million-dollar cat rumor that Ruby had mentioned. Surely no one had taken that seriously.

It was two-thirty when he pulled into the nearly empty parking lot in front of the law office. Pulling his trench coat over his head to block the rain, he ran up to the front door and, since it was locked, banged desperately on it. Surely the assistant hadn't gone home already.

"Sorry," she said as she let him into the foyer. "I'm supposed to lock the door when I'm the only one here." She thrust a large white envelope toward him. "The checks and everything are in here."

He thanked her and wished her Merry Christmas, then ran back out to his car. His plan was to go to Gram's house first. He'd dump his stuff, nuke a microwave meal, then be off to play Santa. But when he drove up to Gram's house, he almost didn't recognize it. First of all, the house was decorated with strings of delicate white lights. And in the front window stood a tall tree, which was lit up as well. Flanking the front door, which had been painted a nice brick red, was a pair of small evergreen trees in shiny red pots. They too were strung with white lights. On the door was a large evergreen wreath with a big plaid bow. Even though he knew that the house was vacant, he couldn't remember when it had ever looked this inviting. So inviting that he entered the house through the front door instead of the back.

Barb was right—he didn't recognize the place. And yet he did. It was the house he'd left behind, only better. It looked so good that he suddenly felt ill at ease, like he was a trespasser. Perhaps he shouldn't be staying there. Just to be sure he called Barb, interrupting her from what sounded like a boisterous Christmas party. He quickly explained and she just laughed.

"Of course you can stay there, darling! It's your house. And, just so you know, most of the agents will be enjoying a break for the next few days. So just make yourself at home and don't worry about messing anything up. Felicia's people will put it all back together. Just enjoy—and Merry Christmas!"

Feeling more relaxed, he dumped his bag in his room, which had also had a facelift. Everything looked amazing. And yet . . . something felt wrong. Something was missing. He glanced around the living room as he headed to the kitchen. Oh yeah . . . no cats. Of course, this simply reminded him of the mission that lay ahead. After putting away a Hungry Man meal, he opened the white envelope and discovered six big checks held together with a paper clip. "Here comes Santa Claus," he said as he slipped them into the inside pocket of his trench coat. Then, feeling unexpectedly merry, he sang the rest of the verse as he crossed the two driveways, hurrying through what was turning into freezing rain, and knocked on Ruby's back door.

"Come in, come in," she called out. "Get yourself outta that cold."

"Merry Christmas, Ruby!" He hugged her tightly.

She returned the greeting, beaming up at him. "I got good news for you."

"What's that?"

"Elliott came back."

"He's here?"

"Not right this minute. He just took off to the store for me. But I expect him back soon." Her face lit up with a huge smile. "Thank you for praying for him. I know you did."

He nodded, reaching into his pocket for the envelope he'd stuck in front. "I sure did. And now I have something for you. Merry Christmas, Ruby."

She fingered the long white envelope with a twinkle in her eye.

"It's not a million dollars," he said quickly.

She laughed. "I didn't think it was."

"But it's from my grandmother. It's for adopting Viola." He glanced around. "How is she?"

Ruby led him to her living room where she had a nice fire burning in the fireplace. "Queen Viola," she proclaimed as she pointed to the beautiful gray cat curled up on a purple velvet cushion. Viola looked up at him with languid green eyes.

He chuckled. "She does look like a queen."

Ruby was opening the envelope. He waited anxiously, hoping that she wouldn't be disappointed. That whole million-dollar-cat story was irritating. But Ruby let out a shriek of delight. "What in tarnation!" She stared at him with big brown eyes. "Is this for real, Garrison Brown? Surely you wouldn't jest with an old woman!"

"It's for real. Merry Christmas. And thanks for taking such good care of Viola."

She hugged him again. "God bless your grandma, Garrison. And God bless you!"

"Now I have some more deliveries to make."

She looked shocked. "Every cat is getting a check?"

He pressed his forefinger to his lips. "Mum's the word, okay?"

She nodded solemnly. He kissed her cheek and patted Viola's head, then made a quick exit. Chuckling to himself, he got into the car. This wasn't so bad!

Next stop was Beth and Annabelle's house. Hopefully they were still home since Beth had mentioned a party they were invited to. He'd called ahead earlier in the week, careful not to tip his hand, but letting them know he would be in town and wanted to make his final visit today. To his relief they were both home and, after checking on Spooky, who seemed perfectly content, he presented them both with the check. The house was filled with squeals of happiness as mother and daughter hugged each other—and then him—dancing around like they'd won the lottery.

Annabelle had Spooky in her arms as he was leaving, gently stroking her. She spoke soothingly in an attempt to calm the cat, who'd been startled by the uproar.

"Merry Christmas," he called out again. "God bless!"

As he got into the car, he realized that the freezing rain was turning into snow. If this kept up they might actually have a white Christmas. Or at least a whitish Christmas. With wipers running, and remembering how unpredictable the Pontiac could be on slick surfaces, he carefully turned the corner and drove down the street to Vincent's house.

To Garrison's surprise and relief, Vincent was not alone on Christmas Eve. "Come in, my friend," Vincent said merrily. Dressed in a cheerful red vest, he nodded toward the living room where several people his age were visiting. "A few of my other friends are here." He held up a small silver cup. "Can I interest you in some eggnog?"

"That sounds good." Garrison slipped off his coat and shook off the snow. "Did you know it's snowing outside?"

"Snow!" Vincent called out to his friends and they let out a cheer.

"How is Rusty?" Garrison asked.

"He's the life of the party." Vincent handed him a cup, nodding toward the living room where a gray-haired woman had the cat on her lap. "He's eating it up." Vincent chuckled. "And how are you? How is Seattle?"

Garrison forced a smile. "Okay." He held out the envelope. "This is a little thank-you from my grandmother—for giving Rusty such a nice home."

Vincent's brows drew together. "What?"

"Open it."

Vincent slowly opened the envelope and removed the check. With wide eyes, he looked at Garrison. "Is this for real?"

Garrison nodded. "Maybe it'll help you with some of those household repairs you've been putting off."

"Oh, my." Vincent's eyes were filled with tears. "I don't know what to say."

"How about *Merry Christmas*?" Garrison set his empty eggnog cup on the dining table and smiled. "Now, if you'll excuse me, I've got a few more deliveries to make before we're all snowed in."

Vincent continued thanking him as he walked him to the door, finally insisting on embracing Garrison before he could leave. Warmed by the eggnog and the gratitude, Garrison proceeded on through the storm. Who knew Christmas could be this much fun? Next stop was Riley and Sabrina's house. Riley answered the door, welcoming him into the house. "What a night, eh?"

"Yeah." Garrison could see that the couple was all dressed up. "Looks like you two are going out?"

"A party at my sister's," Sabrina said with a frown. "Don't get me wrong—I love my sister dearly."

"It's just that she's got three kids under the age of four," Riley explained. "It gets pretty loud."

"Especially tonight." Sabrina pointed to a couple of heaping bags by the door. They were filled with brightly wrapped gifts. "My family always opens on Christmas Eve. It'll be a madhouse."

"At least we can leave," Riley reminded her.

She nodded with a relieved expression. "I know you want to check on Oreo." She glanced over her shoulder. "Last I saw him he was playing with his jingle-bell mouse in the kitchen." She called out, "Here, kitty-kitty," and the black-and-white cat came running. "There's my baby." She bent down to scoop him up. "Mommy and Daddy won't be gone long, sweetheart," she cooed into his happy-looking face. "Be thankful we're not taking you with us. Bentley would probably just jerk you by the tail." She made an exasperated look. "My sister's middle child is in his terrible twos."

Garrison reached over to stroke Oreo's head then reached into his coat pocket. "This is a little thank-you from my grandmother," he told them as he handed it to Riley. "For giving Oreo such a good home."

"What?" Sabrina's eyes grew wide. "Don't tell me that rumor about the million-dollar cat is true?"

Garrison laughed. "No. That is only a rumor. Sorry." He nodded to Riley. "Go ahead and open it."

"Ten thousand dollars?" Riley looked genuinely shocked. "Am I being punked?"

"No." Garrison laughed harder. "This is real. Merry Christmas."

"For taking in a cat?" Riley said. "For real?"

"Not just any cat," Sabrina reminded him. "This is a very special cat."

Riley grinned at her. "I'll say. He is one very special cat." He vigorously shook Garrison's hand. "Thanks, bro!"

Garrison made his exit and then, bracing himself for the next stop, he drove toward David and Jackson's house. The reason he was dreading this visit was because of Cara. He was determined not to look at her house. Just deliver the check and continue on his way. End of story.

Jackson answered the door. "Dad's in the kitchen," he said without too much discomfort.

"How about Muzzy?" Garrison asked. "Where's she?"

"In here." Jackson led Garrison into the living room where Muzzy was sitting beneath a tall, glittering Christmas tree. "She likes to whack the ornaments. I put the ones that break up high so she can't reach."

"Good for you." Garrison kneeled down to pet Muzzy. "You're still a gorgeous girl," he said. She let out several loud meows as if to confirm this.

"Are you staying for Christmas?" Jackson asked.

"No. I just came to drop something by for your dad."

"Garrison," David exclaimed as he came into the living room. "How are you doing?"

"Great." Garrison stood and shook his hand. "Looks like Muzzy is just fine."

David nodded. "Yep. No problems."

Garrison reached into his pocket for the envelope, handing it to David. "This is a thank-you from my grandmother—for taking in Muzzy."

"Huh?" David studied the envelope.

"Go ahead," Garrison encouraged. Reaching over to ruffle Jackson's curly hair, he added, "It's for both of you."

"No way." David held the check in the air. "Are you kidding me?"

Garrison shook his head.

"Wow." David stared at the check. "I'm stunned."

"Merry Christmas," Garrison said, turning to leave.

"So do you have plans for Christmas?" David asked suddenly.

"Well, I—"

"Dad is cooking turkey," Jackson said with enthusiasm. "Cara is coming too."

At the name *Cara*, Garrison froze. "I need to go see someone," he said awkwardly. "But thanks for the invite."

"Sure." David still looked shocked as he held the check in his hand. "And thanks for this."

Garrison gulped in the cold air outside, trying to forget what they'd just said . . . that Cara was spending Christmas with them. Well, of course, she was. Why shouldn't she? Without looking over toward the gingerbread house, he climbed back into the Pontiac. One last stop—and it was only a few blocks away—and then he could go home . . . to his lovely but lonely house.

15

The Maxwells' place was easy to spot—even from a couple blocks away. With so many strings of lights on their house, Garrison hated to imagine their electric bill next month. Maybe this check would help. His plan was to get in and get out ASAP. The less interaction with Handsome Harry, the better. Just the thought of looking into those pale green eyes was unnerving. In and out—and then go home.

"Hello?" A tall, sandy-haired woman answered the door. Behind her was the sound of jarring music, a video game that was turned too loud, and, in Garrison's opinion, total turmoil. "Can I help you?"

"Are you Mrs. Maxwell?" he asked, hoping that he'd come to the wrong house.

"Yes. Do I know you?"

He quickly introduced himself. "I'm the one who gave Harry to your husband a few weeks ago."

"Harry?" she said absently.

"*A large Maine Coon cat*," he said with growing concern. "About three weeks ago."

"Oh, you mean Snoop-Cat."

"Snoop-Cat?" Garrison was confused—and irritated.

"Well, his name was Harry when he got here," she said. "But TJ—that's my oldest—he decided to name him Snoop-Cat. Cute huh?"

Controlling himself, he made a stiff smile. "So, is he—is Snoop-Cat here?"

She gave him a puzzled look. "Sorry, he's not."

"He's not here?"

"No." She grimly shook her head. "Truth is we haven't seen him for—TJ," she yelled loudly, "when was the last time you saw Snoop-Cat?"

A preadolescent boy wearing braces came to the door, examining Garrison with a dull expression. "Huh?"

"Snoop-Cat. When did you last see him?"

"I dunno. Awhile back. Last week maybe."

"Last week?" Garrison felt a wave of panic. "Where did he go?"

"Who knows?" She tipped her head to the chaos going on behind her. "I can barely keep track of these kids—and then their friends come over—honestly, does this look like a house that could keep track of a cat?"

"So you have no idea where Harry went?" Garrison demanded.

The woman rolled her eyes. "God only knows why Tom thought we needed a cat. I thought he'd lost his mind."

"Dad got us the cat to get the money," TJ told her. "Remember?"

She laughed sarcastically. "Oh yeah. That's right. Tommy Boy got it into his head that he was taking in a million-dollar cat." She fixed her eyes on Garrison with an alarmed expression. "That wasn't true, was it?"

"No, no, of course not. Please, excuse me," he said quickly. "I've got to go."

"Wait a minute—was it true?" She followed him out to the porch. "Please, tell me it wasn't true." As Garrison hurried through the fast-falling snow, he could still hear the woman yelling, telling her son how she was going to "kill Tom when he got home."

Inside the protection of the car, Garrison thought about Harry. Good grief, who could blame the poor cat from running away from that madhouse? Garrison would've hit the trail too. But where would Harry have run to? He hadn't gone home. Garrison was sure of that. He'd been through the house. And he'd been to see Ruby—surely she would have told him if Harry had come back.

Garrison put down all the windows of his car, slowly cruising through the neighborhood, calling out Harry's name over and over. Okay, he knew this was ridiculous. How likely was it that Harry would be out roaming the streets in weather like this? Or would he? Garrison drove all around, going down every street and even a few alleys until he got worried that he might be disturbing some of the neighbors.

Fearful that Harry had been injured somehow, he pulled over and got out his phone, dialing information and getting the numbers of the local veterinarians. He called each of them, inquiring about missing Maine Coon cats whenever a live person answered and leaving a message with his number when they didn't. Wherever Harry was—Garrison was determined to find him.

With the windows open, snow had blown into the car and, despite the heater running full bore, Garrison was chilled to the bone. "Oh, Harry," he said desperately as he turned toward Gram's house, "please, come home, old boy. I'm sorry I gave you to those horrid people. I didn't know they were like that." And then, although he knew some would declare it wrong to pray for an animal—he didn't care what they thought—he shot up an earnest prayer on Harry's behalf. He made no apologies as he begged God to keep his furry friend safe and to bring him home.

He parked the Pontiac in the driveway and cranked up all the windows. Then, since he was already cold and wet, he did a quick trip around the perimeter of the house, calling out Harry's name. He even checked in Gram's garden shed. But no Harry.

Feeling like he'd lost his best friend, Garrison went back into the house and peeled off his wet coat, hanging it by the kitchen door. Then, remembering the check, he removed it from his coat pocket. It would need to be returned to Mr. Miller.

Thinking of Gram's MIA attorney was troubling. How was it possible that Mr. Miller had totally forgotten the "surprise visit" to the Maxwells'? Garrison knew that if Mr. Miller had gone as promised, he never would have approved that family. Indeed, if he'd gone, he likely would have discovered Harry was missing back then.

Garrison was just putting the check back in the large white envelope when he realized there was a slender folder inside. He pulled it out to discover it contained the title to the house and a couple of envelopes. He recognized Gram's lacy handwriting on the first envelope. Feeling a lump in his throat—and as if he'd let her down—he slowly opened it, removing several pages of fine stationery.

Dear Garrison,

If you are reading this, I must be departed to my heavenly home. I felt rather certain that my time was near. For that reason I've met with Mr. Miller, but you must know that by now. First of all, my dear boy, I want to tell you how much I love you. I fear that you may temporarily misinterpret my devotion to you because of my desire to find my cats good homes. So I want you to know that, along with my dear husband and son, you have been one of the loves of my life. You may not know how lost I felt when you came to me. I was grieving for your grandfather and for leaving Kenya. And then I was grieving for your father. But you brought life back to me. Your youth and energy forced me to participate in the community. I got involved in your school and church and the neighborhood. You, my dear boy, brought me back to life.

But when you went back east to college, I felt a bit lost again. I missed you more than you will ever know and I did not want you to know. That is when I got a cat. Genevieve was a wonderful companion to me. I was aware of your allergies and I knew I'd willingly find the dear cat a new home if you chose to come back, but I suspected that you would not. Then, when you went to Uganda (which made me so happy) I got another cat. Well, you know how this story goes. One good cat led to another. But I never went out looking for them. No, they came to me. And while you were so far away, they were my family.

Because you are reading this I know that you have successfully found good homes for all six of my "children." I thank you for that, Garrison. You may have guessed that one part of my plan was to keep you in your old neighborhood for a spell. I hoped that you might reconnect and perhaps even discover where it is the Good Lord is leading you next. I have to say that you've sounded a bit lost in our phone conversations. But I understand that. I felt lost too.

Now, lest you think I loved my cats more than I loved you, you will find another envelope in this package that Mr. Miller has prepared in the event of my demise. In that package you will find the title to my house and a check for the remainder of my inheritance. As you can see, you are receiving a much greater portion than the kitties. I know that you will use the money wisely—to help yourself and your fellow man. I pray that it will be a blessing and not a curse. Most of all I pray that you will find someone as dear to you as your grandfather was to me. It is hard to go this life alone. But if you must, perhaps you should get yourself a dog.

Always remember that your heavenly Father and your grandmother are watching over you, dear Garrison.

All my love,
Gram

With tears in his eyes, Garrison opened up the last envelope and removed a cashier's check. He stared at the figure, then, blinking to clear his eyes, he looked again. No, he was not a millionaire, but it was more money than Garrison could possibly earn in ten years. He shook his head in disbelief. But as he slid the check back into the envelope he felt unworthy of it. After all, it was his fault that one of Gram's beloved cats was missing. Sure, he knew she would understand and forgive him. She'd have to forgive her attorney too. As did Garrison.

Even so, Garrison wasn't sure he could forgive himself. How had he been so shortsighted? Why hadn't he investigated the Maxwells more carefully on that first day? And why had he left Harry—of all the cats—with what appeared to be a "gold digging" family? Poor Harry!

Still feeling chilled and blue, he went into the living room, and seeing that some birch logs were laid in the fireplace, probably for show, he struck a long match to light them, watching as the papery bark slowly caught fire. And not wanting to turn on the lights, he decided to light the candles along the mantel as well. It seemed a little silly to light candles with no one else around to enjoy them, but he hoped that it would put him in a better Christmas spirit.

In an attempt to distract himself from obsessing over Harry, he tried to focus his attention on the changes Barb had made to the house. Really, it was amazing, and perfect for Christmas, even if it was an illusion. The house truly looked festive—as if it should be hosting friends gathering around food with Christmas tunes playing in the background. He wished he could feel as festive as his surroundings looked.

He tried to recall the happy faces he'd witnessed while delivering the unexpected checks around the neighborhood. Surely his stint as "Santa" should be enough to erase the

Christmas Scrooge feelings that were darkening his heart. He reminded himself of his own check. Anyone else receiving a windfall like that would probably be over the moon.

He held his hands over the crackling flames, remembering Gram's sweet letter and how she'd wanted him to know how much she loved him. Okay, that warmed his heart. No denying it. But thinking of Gram reminded him of the cats . . . and how he'd let her down. How he'd let Harry down. Suddenly he felt blue again.

He could hear car doors closing out front. Glancing out, he watched as several people got out and hurried up to Ruby's house. She always hosted Christmas for her relatives, packing them into her little house and stuffing them with all the good foods she'd been preparing for days. Ruby had always included Gram and him as well, and he knew he would be welcome there tonight. He also knew he was in no condition to put on his game face and make small talk. Better to just lay low.

If he got hungry, he could nuke another microwave meal. He'd probably go to bed early and try to sleep. Perhaps he'd hear from one of the veterinarians tomorrow. If not, he would post "missing cat" signs all over town. He'd even offer a generous reward. That should help stir things up.

He was just heading for the kitchen when he heard the doorbell. Had one of Ruby's guests mistaken this house for hers? He hurried to open it, ready to redirect them next door, when to his surprise he saw Cara. With her bright red scarf circling her neck and white lacy flakes falling on her dark hair, she was truly a vision. For a moment he almost thought he was halucinating. But it was what she held in her arms that made him blink twice. Was this for real?

"*Harry!*" he exclaimed, reaching for the long-lost cat. "It's you!"

"Hello, Garrison," Cara said with an uneasy expression.

"Cara, hello! You found Harry!"

"Yes."

"Harry, old boy." Garrison held the cat close, looking down into his face. "I was so worried about you. I looked all over the neighborhood. I'm so glad you're okay." Suddenly he looked back at Cara. "I'm sorry. Do you want to come in?"

"Sure, if you don't mind."

"Not at all." He opened the door wide. "Come in and get warm. I even made a fire." He closed the door and set Harry down, then took her coat and led her to the fireplace.

"The house looks great," she said quietly.

"Yeah. Do you want to see the whole thing? I can turn the lights on and—"

"I've actually seen it already," she confessed. "I slipped in while your real estate agent was doing the open house."

"Right . . ." Garrison bent down and picked up Harry again. "I can't believe you found him, Cara. How did you? Where did you? When did you?"

"One question at a time," she said patiently. "I was on one of my regular afternoon walks several days ago. I was passing a vacant house on Washington Street—you know that old Victorian that's in really bad shape?"

"Yeah. The old Brinson place."

"Anyway I thought I saw a cat on the porch. I thought that was weird since no one lived there. And, as you know, I've been wanting a cat. As I walked up to the porch, I thought it was probably a feral cat because it looked kind of matted and straggly and wet, but it had been raining. I called out 'here, kitty-kitty' and it came running toward me. At first I was kind of worried—what if it had rabies or something? Then I looked into those green eyes and I thought it looked just like Harry, but I didn't think that was possible."

"Wow . . . amazing . . ."

"Anyway I took him home and dried him off and fed him. He was really hungry." She shrugged. "He's been with me ever since."

"When did you figure out it was Harry?"

"I tried to tell myself it wasn't really Harry," she said a bit sheepishly. "Like maybe he was Harry's long-lost brother, you know?"

"Uh-huh . . ." He scratched Harry's chin.

"But then I called him by his name—Harry." She made a sad smile. "And he came running. I knew then."

"Really? He came to you, just like that?"

"I tried to call you, Garrison. I tried your cell phone and the phone here at the house. But they were both out of service."

He explained that he'd changed numbers.

"And the reason I sneaked into the open house was to ask your agent how to reach you. But she was talking with a couple who looked like serious buyers and I didn't want to distract her." She frowned. "I was pretty disappointed when I saw the For Sale sign, Garrison. Didn't see that one coming."

"I'm thinking about taking that sign down," he confessed.

She looked surprised. "Anyway, when I went over to David's tonight, I heard that you'd been by. Heard about the check you gave him." She smiled. "That was really generous. He can use it right now. Starting his home business has been a challenge."

"Well, that was my grandmother's doing. I was just the delivery boy."

"Anyway, I thought I'd better get Harry back to you."

"Thank you!" He explained about the Maxwells.

"That's terrible."

"Yeah. I would much rather have given Harry to you." He reminded her of the conditions of Gram's will. "If I could've I would've, Cara."

"That's okay. I understand." She pointed at him. "Hey, what about your allergies? Or have you already taken some medicine?"

He looked down at Harry. "No, I haven't taken anything today. But, you're right, I don't seem to be sneezing . . . yet . . ."

They both just stood by the crackling fire without speaking. Garrison didn't know what to say. But he wished he could think of a reason to entice her to stay. "Sorry I can't offer you any Christmas goodies . . . I haven't even been to the store yet."

"That's okay. I should get back to David's. Besides, you probably have something to do . . . I mean, for Christmas Eve."

"No, no, not really." He could feel Harry getting restless in his arms and so he set him back down, watching as the handsome cat sauntered around, exploring the room with feline interest.

"But, um, before I go," she spoke slowly, "I'd like to ask you a question."

"Go for it." He folded his arms across his chest, studying her closely. He wanted to memorize the curve of her cheek, the way her dark eyes sparkled in the firelight, the fullness of her lips, the way she tipped her head to one side as she spoke.

"Okay . . . so I just want to know, Garrison Brown—why didn't you tell me goodbye?"

"Goodbye?"

"Yeah, you left here without even telling me you were going. And, call me stupid, but I thought we were friends."

"We were friends," he declared. "I mean, we *are* friends. Aren't we?"

"I guess. But, well . . . I just thought we had, uh, maybe something more. *You know?*" Her eyes narrowed with uncertainty. "But I must've been wrong. Otherwise you wouldn't have taken off like that—without a word."

"I thought you and David were a couple," he said abruptly.

"Me and David?" Her brow creased. *"Seriously?"*

"Yeah." He nodded sincerely. "You went to that Christmas party with him and—"

"I had agreed to do that a couple weeks before I even knew you, Garrison. In fact, I'm pretty sure I told you about it. David had this big fancy work-related party to attend and he didn't want to go stag. It was nothing. Absolutely nothing."

"What about the Christmas parade? You and David and Jackson together—you all looked pretty cozy, just like a happy little family."

She let out an exasperated sigh. "I had offered to take Jackson to the parade because David couldn't. It was going to be just Jackson and me and Santa Claus. David was tied up with a client coming by his house to look at something. Then his client was a no-show and David surprised me with coffee. You were there, you saw it."

"I saw it . . . but I guess I misunderstood," he admitted. Had he really been that off base, that thickheaded—to put a completely wrong spin on everything? "But what about tonight?" he said suddenly.

"Tonight?" She ran her hands down the sides of her dress,

a crinkly, cranberry-colored velveteen that was very pretty on her. She slipped her hands into pockets, waiting for him to explain himself.

"You're going to spend Christmas Eve with David and Jackson. I know it because they both told me. David is cooking a turkey. And you should probably be there with them right now." He proclaimed this like *"Aha, I got you!"* Although he'd never wanted anything less.

"Yes, I probably should be there right now," she confessed. "Along with a couple dozen other people."

"A couple dozen?" Garrison felt an irrational rush of hope. "So David's having a dinner party?"

"That's right. A potluck actually. Mostly people from the neighborhood. Some that you know as a matter of fact. Beth and Annabelle are coming. So are Sabrina and Riley—as soon as she can extract herself from her sister's house."

"Interesting . . ." Really interesting.

"So do you want to go with me or not?" she demanded playfully. "The food should be good—a lot better than your microwave meal. I made a big ol' pan of real mac and cheese—used three cheeses."

"Yeah, sure. Sounds great." He nodded in disbelief. "But, by *going with you* . . . do you mean kind of like a date?"

Her eyes twinkled merrily. "Kinda like that."

"Okay!"

"But not so fast, Mr. Brown." She pulled what looked like a small piece of a plant from her pocket. Was it from the poinsettia? She dangled it in front of him.

"What's that?" he asked.

She held it over her head. "Mistletoe."

He grinned with realization. "You mean . . . ?"

"Oh yeah . . ." She leaned forward with an expectant expression.

Garrison took in a quick breath, then leaned down toward her and, gazing into her eyes, he kissed her—and she definitely kissed him back! When they finally stepped away, he could feel the room spinning around him.

"Merry Christmas, Garrison," she whispered.

"Yeah," he said in a husky voice. *"Merry Christmas!"*

Melody Carlson is the award-winning author of over two hundred books, including *Christmas at Harrington's*, *The Christmas Pony*, and *A Simple Christmas Wish*. Melody recently received a Romantic Times Career Achievement Award in the inspirational market for her books. She and her husband live in central Oregon. For more information about Melody, visit her website at www.melodycarlson.com.

Meet Melody at

MelodyCarlson.com

- Enter a contest for a signed book
- Read her monthly newsletter
- Find a special page for book clubs
- Discover more books by Melody

Become a fan on Facebook

Melody Carlson Books